She could feel his breath on her cheek and trembled.

"Are you afraid of me?"

"Of course not, it is just all too much. It is all happening too fast. I can barely think."

His hand went to her cheek. "I am sorry. I want you to accept the marriage as the best for us. There is much we have in common. I am beginning to agree with Blanche, who thinks you are the best possible match for me."

Her eyes widened. "Really?"

"Really," he said, and bent his head. He placed a kiss somewhere between her lips and cheek, for Eugenia had turned her head when he leaned toward her. His hand cupped her chin, the other circled her waist, and he kissed her. She found herself kissing him back.

He stepped back and smiled. Crinkles appeared at the corners of his eyes, which flashed with amusement. "Now, that was not too distasteful, I trust."

"Not in the least, my lord."

SCANDALOUS JOURNEY

Roberta Eckert

FAWCETT CREST • NEW YORK

A Fawcett Crest Book
Published by Ballantine Books
 Published in the United States by Ballantine Books, a division of Random House, Inc., New York, and simultaneously in Canada by Random House of Canada Limited, Toronto.

Library of Congress Catalog Card Number: 92-90603

ISBN 0-449-22179-2

Manufactured in the United States of America

First Edition: December 1992

To Heidi
My golden girl, second
born and loving friend.

One

Eugenia Dudley was better off than most orphans who lived in neglect, misery, and crowded conditions throughout England in 1810. She, at least, was housed in a private school by the generosity of Richard Winslow, the seventh Earl of Grahame.

Her father, Captain Dudley, had fallen in battle against the Dutch settlement on Ceylon in 1796. Before he died, he had asked Lord Grahame to see to the welfare of his daughter, who would face life as an orphan. Lord Grahame had not yet come into his honors, but did so in 1797, and upon his return to England he kept his word to his comrade in arms.

He had sworn an oath to her dying father to see that Eugenia was educated and then settled with a husband. Honor required that the earl keep this pledge since Captain Dudley had, after all, saved his own life many years earlier. He had found the child in the care of a distant cousin of Dudley's, who was only too relieved to relinquish the child. The earl was first a military man, and he, being widowed, had decided it would be best to place the child in a school. He had certainly lacked time for the child, and his own son was at school.

On the recommendation of friends who knew

about such things, the seventh Earl of Grahame had placed Miss Dudley in the Addington School for Young Ladies. The name was a misnomer. In actuality, it was an institution for castoff children of all ages. Babes born on the wrong side of the blanket and orphans whose relatives did not care to raise them were sent to live in this drafty converted priory. The exorbitant fee for discretion and convenience was paid and the children all but forgotten.

The earl generously arranged for money to be sent for Eugenia's education, and as she grew older, a small stipend was included each quarter. She became a mere obligation to be attended to by his lordship's man of business. No one ever called to see how she fared. Since few children were visited, she did not consider this lack amiss.

Eugenia had acquired the necessary skills for survival in such a place. She learned early on to be wary of people and observe them carefully, reserving any opinion until she could be certain of its accuracy.

Recognizing her intellect to be her only source of power, she applied herself with diligence and, in doing so, found a genuine love of learning. Therefore, what began as an escape from her surroundings became the focus of her existence.

With the stipend sent to her by the earl, she purchased books. Eugenia taught herself Latin, Greek, and English classics. She became remarkably well educated. It was her only solace beyond the joy of caring for the babies and little ones.

Over the years Eugenia gained an astounding education. This had been encouraged by Miss Smythe, the headmistress, who put the girl to tutoring the younger students as soon as she realized Eugenia's intellect. Miss Smythe was delighted to have an unpaid teacher. As Eugenia grew, she was given more teaching responsibilities and became indispensable to the staff.

On this cold, cold day Eugenia Dudley drew her shawl tightly around her shoulders and slowed her steps at the doorway. Frowning when she heard the rasping cough of several children, she glanced around the drafty room. It was fine for a priory and those who believed sacrifice and austerity were tributes to God, but it was no place for children. The walls were gray stone and the high fan-vaulted ceilings proclaimed its Gothic heritage. High windows with stone tracery let in a weak winter light on which tiny dust motes gave the room a misty quality.

She shook her head in dismay: This was no place for the children. She adored them. They were always a pleasure, and she had devoted as much time as possible to them. Squeals of delight and laughter from the children echoed in the large room, for they loved her. She stooped to gather as many in her arms as was possible.

"How are my darlings today?" she asked, making sure her voice was heard above all the clamor. There was magic in her laughter and in her shining eyes. The children turned their faces to her as flowers to the sun.

"Sing to us," one said.

"No, you promised a story."

She picked up Nell and kissed her. "Let's wipe that runny nose," she said, taking a handkerchief from her apron. She set the child on her lap. "We'll have our story, and take turns," she said, pulling another child onto her other knee and winking at the rest. They giggled. Some sat, others stood, enthralled by the only brightness in their lives.

Eugenia's eyes scanned their upturned faces, and her heart broke. How could she leave them? Tears threatened, but if ever in her life she must meet a challenge, it was now. She could not, must not, cry.

It was at that moment that the headmistress, Miss Smythe, entered. It was an unwelcome interruption and Eugenia frowned slightly. The woman always seemed to be an interruption, Eugenia thought as she gazed at the stalwart-looking woman with pale, watery eyes and thin gray hair severely pinned into a bun. Her step was heavy and purposeful as she strode into the room, out of breath and decidedly in panic. This state resulted in her purple-flushed face and bulging veins at her temples. Not a pretty sight.

"He's here, he's here!"

"Who is here?" Eugenia asked evenly.

"Don't provoke me. You know perfectly well . . . I mean . . . the Earl of Grahame!" Miss Smythe spoke with no effort taken to hide her irritation. This chit always annoyed her, and she would be glad to see the back of her. Yes, she would miss her teaching help and the earl's quarterly board payments, which were generous enough to filch some for herself, but she would not miss the knowing irony in Eugenia Dudley's eyes.

"Do hurry. He's waiting. Why are you dressed so?"

Eugenia smiled sweetly. "I'm always dressed like this. Why do you ask?"

"You know perfectly well what I mean. You

should have put on your brown wool with the lace collar."

"It will make no difference what I wear. Besides, don't you think I should save my best dress for Sunday services? We wouldn't want the earl to think I lacked a Sunday dress, now, would we?" Her voice was soft and carried no obvious disdain, but the implication was not lost on Miss Smythe.

The headmistress shrugged. "I have done my best for you," she added defensively, wishing she had been forewarned by the earl. She could have provided a new gown for Miss Dudley. How like the gentry to appear—out of the blue—and expect instant attention. It was a worry and she hoped she would not be censured for the pitiful way Miss Dudley looked. She comforted herself with the thought that nothing could be done to improve the girl. Providence had decreed Miss Dudley's appearance, and how could she presume to question God's work?

"Do hurry. Lord Grahame is waiting in the antechamber." Miss Smythe turned and left the room.

Eugenia's eyes rested on the empty space left by the woman's departure. With a sigh and glistening tears she turned to the children still clinging to her skirts. How could she leave them? Who would love them? Murmuring words of comfort, she picked each up in turn and kissed their dear faces.

"I shall come to see you again, I promise." But could she?

They cried and clung. Dear God, she prayed, let me help them. Kissing each again, she left the room without looking back, for to do so would be her undoing.

Her laggard steps and slumped shoulders reflected the heaviness of the burden in her heart.

Yes, the Earl of Grahame had come to fetch her and fulfill the promise made to her dying father. She scoffed at the thought. His efforts to date could hardly be considered any encumbrance, but now he apparently had stirred himself enough to come and take her from this dreary place.

He was to see her settled. She scorned the idea. He must be too old to bother with a ward, let alone find her a husband. The implications of being saddled with some nondescript husband chosen for her boded an ominous future. Would she have a say in the choice? A shiver of distaste ran through her body.

Yet, a timid glimmer of joy at the thought of leaving this dank place surfaced despite the crushing sadness of leaving the children. Despite the grim reality of the drafty priory, it was all she had known, but now the unfamiliar world took on a paradoxical aspect. Life beyond these walls beckoned with an allure as the land of Pester John had for the crusaders.

Her steps enlivened at the idea of leaving, and she hurried through the long corridors and up several flights of stairs to her bedchamber. The tiny room was in a small corner on the third floor and had been given to her when she became a staff member. At Miss Smythe's insistence, she was separated from the children when she began full-time teaching. The room was her haven and she had spent hours there contentedly reading and dreaming.

She closed the door and leaned against it, shutting it against the world in a fleeting feeling of safety. She lingered in the sensation for some moments, as if to hold the waiting world at bay. A distant clock chimed, rudely forcing her thoughts to her task at hand. She glanced around the small room and knew she must gather her belongings. Her possessions were few but some very dear.

Taking a deep breath, she pushed away from the door. First, she removed the small velvet case from the dresser drawer. The little jewel case held her mother's cameo and a precious miniature of her mother wearing the lovely cameo.

As a child Eugenia spent hours looking at the cameo and miniature, trying to preserve the image of her beautiful mother in her fading memories. She had clung tenaciously to the image, and soon the cameo blended with the miniature as likenesses of her mother. It had given her comfort in the long gray years that followed in dulling numbers. She placed her links to the past into her waiting valise.

While the years had been bleak, Eugenia had made the best of them in the endeavors she had taken upon herself. She had ceased being a child when she entered this school at the age of eight. She was wise beyond her one and twenty years, for there existed in her soul nothing of the child. While she could charm and delight children, that talent came from love, not from the joy of a youthful outlook.

Granted, her thoughts sometimes were filled with sheltered dreams that bordered on mere fairy tales. These had been only a means of escape. Such thoughts were hidden, since she lived in the world where had they been known, she would have been forced to relinquish them. She did not recognize this aspect and would have vehemently denied the idea if presented to her.

Although not frightened to meet the earl, she

trembled with trepidation at what life might hold outside the confining school walls. She understood life here and could control the events around her, or at least exist within them.

Giving over her belongings to the handyman who came to take them to the earl's coach, she picked up her shawl and draped it about her shoulders. Drawing it tight, as if to protect herself, she closed her eyes for a moment and took a deep breath to steel herself.

Lord Thomas Winslow, the eighth Earl of Grahame, stood motionless, silently staring out the window of the ancient priory that now housed the Addington School for Young Ladies. By current standards, he was not a handsome man; there was nothing of the Byronic about him. Still, his manly form could not be faulted, because he was tall, broad-shouldered, and carried himself with a proud bearing. His rich brown hair was sprinkled with gray strands at his temples and curled unfashionably long on his collar. His profile proclaimed his family lineage back to the Romans. The planes of his face were hard and his brows a fierce slash over icy gray eyes. Lord Grahame's only claim to softness of facial character was expressed in his sensual mouth.

There was an easy air in his countenance with no hint of the dandy in his dress. While his attire was tailored of fine fabric, it was worn with a casual indifference. His high-top boots were even spattered with mud-soiled snow.

An inadequate fire flickered in the great Tudor fireplace, offering no comfort other than the illusion of warmth in the sight of its meager flames.

His capped coat did not ward off the chill that permeated his body.

Shifting his weight, he absently rubbed his aching thigh, which was a souvenir of Talavera de la Reina. He swore a silent oath. Inclement weather inevitably brought back the aches of that wound.

His breath hung on the cold air in misted crystals as he gazed at the splayed fingers of frost that spiked their way across the window glass. Damn, he thought, and his pale gray eyes flashed with impatience. He had been kept standing in this frozen antechamber for what seemed like an eon. He had miles to travel with the child, and the barest hint of winter sun clung perilously low on the horizon. There were not many hours of daylight left. He turned sharply at the sound of the opening door.

The bracket-faced headmistress entered the room with a mouse of a girl in her wake. Lord Grahame's eyes narrowed in dismay as he took in her appearance. His ward was no child! She was a young lady dressed in a loose-fitting wool gown of some putrid color that hovered between brown and pea green. She clutched a gray wool shawl about her shoulders. Her drab brown hair was plaited and wrapped around her head. With eyes lowered in obvious trepidation and reluctance, she trailed behind the daunting headmistress.

"Lord Grahame, here is your ward, Miss Dudley."

Grahame could not hide his shock. Great heavens, not only is she not a child, he thought, she is without any apparent charm. Good God, he was responsible for seeing her settled! Penniless, homely, and meek she was. What a herculean task. Overwhelmed at once, he rebelled at this duty placed on him by his father's will. His glare never left the submissive Eugenia Dudley as she crossed the empty space.

The chit, who was now his ward, stood before him and slowly raised her eyes. A tremor ran through his body. Gazing into the biggest, most beautiful hazel eyes he had ever beheld, he suddenly felt as if he had been ambushed. His frown deepened.

Miss Smythe shifted with a nervous twitch. "Lord Grahame, may I present your ward, Eugenia Dudley?" She repeated the sentence, then waited.

The barest nod indicated his acknowledgment, and a reluctant one at that.

Eugenia, who had lived in apprehension from the moment she first learned she was to leave the school in the care of the Earl of Grahame, trembled. How strange, the earl is much younger than she expected! She had assumed he would be much older since he had been a military comrade to her father. How could this be? Judging the expression on his face, she instinctively saw the earl disliked her.

She dropped him a curtsy. "How do you do, my lord?"

He again nodded. "Do you have your belongings ready?"

"Everything but my books. May I please take them?"

Grahame looked to Miss Smythe, who was frowning with annoyance. "She has dozens of them," she said, as if such ownership constituted some crime.

"I'll have them sent for. Is that agreeable, Miss Smythe, Miss Dudley?"

"But of course," murmured the headmistress.

Miss Dudley's answer consisted of a smile as

bright as the June sunshine. It came suddenly and disappeared just as quickly.

Damn, from bad to worse, she's a bluestocking to boot. The husband-to-be faded further from the realm of possibility. Maybe, he thought, he could find a curate for her.

Two

Eugenia lowered her head and covered her mouth against the cold air and buffeting wind that accosted them as they left the old priory. Pulling her cape closer, she tried to shield herself against the onslaught. The footing was treacherous, and she minced her sliding steps.

Seeing her difficulty, Grahame grabbed her arm to steady her, only to find his own footing less than sure. He put his arm about her and held her from falling.

She could feel the hardness of his muscled arm as he pulled her close and was grateful for his strength. They clung, holding each other up as they negotiated the ice-rutted walk.

Ben, the earl's coachman, was pacing impatiently. "I'd about given you up! I've kept the cattle moving as best I could, but we had best be off."

Grahame nodded. "I was kept waiting. I judge the establishment to be sadly lacking. It is getting late and I am uneasy about making Windhaven by nightfall."

The coachman looked around at the blowing snow and cocked an eyebrow in agreement. He swung up onto the box to ready the team into motion.

Grahame had total faith in the ability of his

coachman, but he was annoyed at the unnecessary delay that now placed them in an uneasy position.

After helping his ward into the coach, the earl offered a fur lap robe to fend off the biting cold. He was not pleased about his obligation, but he did not want the ill-clad girl to die of some lung affliction acquired on this frightful day. He shook his head as he climbed into the well-sprung coach, knowing he had chosen the worst possible day on which to fetch Miss Dudley.

Taking the seat opposite her, he signaled the coachman to proceed. Settling back, he studied his ward. Her eyes were lowered and her hands demurely folded on her lap. Feeling his scrutiny, she glanced up to him in an open, frank stare which took him by surprise. The pose was so demure, and the gaze so candid, he felt disarmed by the incongruity.

The earl knew nothing about raising young ladies, and it was a damn good thing his sister had agreed to take the girl off his hands. Of course, that was before he learned she was full-grown. Blanche would *have* to take her now. As a bachelor, he certainly couldn't keep her in his establishment.

He broke the silence with a commonplace remark. "What an unfortunate day to travel!"

Eugenia nodded agreement from the warmth of the fur blanket. "However, I think any day one could leave that school could only be considered glorious."

Lord Grahame did not know how to respond, since it was his father who had put her there. He made no reply, and they fell into silence as the coach moved along in slow monotony.

She dropped her eyes and regretted her remark

in the event he thought it a criticism of the choice in schools. It was too bold and not the truth. She hated leaving the children, all that was familiar, and to what her future might bode could be far worse. She bit her lip and vowed to keep her counsel. It would not do for him to think her ungrateful.

The flurries continued obliterating the world in a vast emptiness of white. The six great bays pulled the coach with increasing difficulty as the snow accumulated. With only a few hours of daylight left, the earl was now sure they could not make Windhaven by nightfall. His jaw tightened as he mentally recounted the inns between their present location and his country seat.

Glancing at the girl, who was sitting as still as a bird on a fence poised for flight, he shrugged. He was getting fanciful in his old age. This thought amused him, and a smile touched the corners of his lips.

Blanche would know what to do, he thought. She would see the chit was groomed and made presentable, though the task seemed insurmountable. There was a small sum held in trust for her dowry, and he would add to it if necessary. It would take a considerable fortune to secure this maid a husband. But he would see to it; after all, it was his duty to do so.

Eugenia kept her eyes carefully averted. He made her nervous. Now and again she would sneak a peek at him. She could feel his animosity. It seethed out of his pores and filled the air. She was sure of it! What a judgmental boor, she thought, not considering her own leap to a first impression. He knew nothing about her, nothing! He is judging by external appearances, and that only confirmed his shallowness. Well, she thought, I hope his wife is an empty-headed beauty—he deserves one.

No matter how he viewed her, the fact remained she was under his charge. May the Lord take mercy upon her. She burrowed deeper into the fur cover. The swaying motion of the coach, despite its fits and starts, lulled her into drowsiness. She closed her heavy eyelids with the soothing thought that it would do no good to worry—yet.

The miles traveled were difficult and the distance covered negligible. Falling snow continued to drift, and the horses struggled to keep the coach moving. Their breathing grew labored with the effort.

The pale gray sky began to fade. To the east, the horizon was already dark. Just as Grahame leaned forward with the intention of ordering the coachman to pull into the nearest inn, the coach came to a quaking halt. The abrupt stop caused Miss Dudley to fly from her seat and land sprawled on the lap of his lordship.

"Allow me, Miss Dudley," he said, struggling to remove her draped body from his own. The moment was embarrassing as he hastily and inelegantly lifted her from his lap.

The sudden halt had been into the side of a snowbank. Ben jumped off the box and rushed to open the door to help the struggling passengers.

With some difficulty Grahame managed to climb out of the tilted coach now resting against a snowbank. His leg hurt like hell. He and Ben quickly assessed the situation. "What do you think?" Grahame asked, kneeling beside his coachman.

"We'll not get out without help, and I fear the wheel on the front left is broken. Can't tell for sure with this snow," Ben answered, trying to brush the packed snow away from the wheel.

"Here, let me help. Maybe we can get it out."

The coachman stood and shook his head. "We can try if you wish, but it could tip. It is very near that now."

Remembering Miss Dudley, Grahame rose from his crouch and walked back to the door. He raised his arms to lift Miss Dudley. "We need to lighten the load," he said. "Although you could make little difference." Lifting her slender body easily off the coach, he took her arm and aided her through the foot-high snow.

She felt the snow top her boots and begin to melt against her leg. The cold water trickled fiendishly slowly down her ankle and along her instep, leaving the inside of her boots cold and wet. Wrinkling her nose at the nasty sensation, she stamped her feet.

Grahame paused and surveyed their surroundings. The landscape grew dimmer in the falling snow and fading light. "I think I can see the lights of the Boar's Head Inn in the distance. Unhitch the team. We cannot keep them standing in this cold weather after all their exertion."

"Your lordship, perhaps I should take a horse and ride to Windhaven for help. I can make it alone in a few hours. We'll not get this coach out, and even if we did, I am sure the wheel is damaged."

"Can you ride that long without a saddle? Is the horse up to a fast ride? They have pulled their load for the day."

"Your lordship, I know my horses. I will take Misty; she's a game one, she is. We'll do just fine."

Grahame nodded agreement. There seemed no other choice. He turned suddenly and rested his eyes on Eugenia, standing huddled in her cape.

"Are you warm enough?" he asked.

"Yes, my lord," she replied, surprised that he thought to ask. She watched him nod, then move away to assist with the unhitching of the team. She had lied. She was cold and getting colder by the moment. Her nose and toes were numb, and her lashes covered with snowflakes.

The men worked with dispatch, and in minutes the team had been unharnessed and the traces dropped. Ben cut the driving reins in order to manage the chosen horse. Next, he covered the animal with a blanket and mounted the horse bareback.

"I'll return by morning with a carriage and new team. I'll bring a crew to get the coach out and the wheel repaired. Can you make the inn by walking, or should ye try to ride bareback with Miss Dudley?"

Eugenia shrank back. The huge horses terrified her. They stamped and snorted, and it was frightening. "I have never been on a horse," she said.

Grahame frowned. "No, no, I think the Boar's Head Inn is just down the road, or I would not be able to see the lights on an evening like this. We'll be fine. Get on with you."

"I'll be back by morning," Ben said, and was off, disappearing into the falling snow.

"We shall be there in short time, you'll see, and then we shall have a nice warm meal." He said this as though to comfort them both. "We need the lantern," Grahame said, and headed toward the coach.

"Here, you carry the fur robe; might even put it around you."

Eugenia obeyed and wrapped the fur around her tightly. It was big and rather awkward, but she'd manage and be grateful for its warmth.

Next, Grahame took out the hamper that held some wine and food. He was pleased Mrs. Henley, his housekeeper, had insisted on sending it along on the journey. He was not sure of the fare at the Boar's Head Inn, and he was always grateful for Lila's cooking.

"We cannot leave my things!" Eugenia cried. "Someone might take them."

Lord Grahame sighed in exasperation. The day had tried his patience beyond any he had known. "I must lead the horses and carry this hamper. You must carry the lanterns, for it is likely to be totally dark before we reach the inn. How do you suggest we carry the luggage?" His voice was as sharp as a knife. He capitulated with another sigh of exasperation. "Very well, I will fetch it." He climbed up onto the coach, and his leg ached with each movement.

"Get the hat box," she commanded.

He turned his face to her and frowned. "Yes, mistress."

Eugenia blushed, but she would have her way in this. She watched him untie the box, bring it down, and hand it to her.

"I will not leave my mother's picture or her cameo," she said with the resolve of Cerberus guarding the gates of Hell.

"How are you going to carry it?" he said, indicating he would not.

"I shall remove the velvet case and put it in the hamper. We can put the box in the coach. Do you think anyone will steal it?"

"On a night like this? If anyone is out on a night like this, they are welcomed to it!"

Eugenia smiled.

"Best we get moving," Grahame said, and took the harness of the lead horse. He set his footsteps toward the flickering light in the distance. The tired team obeyed, enlivened a little by the lack of the heavy coach.

Eugenia scampered alongside the tall earl, careful to keep him between her and the monstrous horses. Now and again she cast a wary glance to those formidable beasts and was grateful she had not had to get upon the back of one. The very idea was terrifying.

Clutching the two lanterns and the huge lap robe, she could see the light in the distance. It faded every now and again in a flurry of snow. The walking became more difficult, for one had to lift one's feet out of the snow with every step and her feet were soaking wet.

She began to pant, and each intake of cold air seared her lungs. Every little while she stopped for a brief second to catch her breath, rub the ache in her side, and shift her burden. *Miserable* would be a lighthearted description of her condition, she mused.

Lord Grahame watched with growing apprehension. His frown deepened, for it was becoming unmistakably clear that he had made his second mistake of the day. He looked at his ward and silently cursed the situation that was becoming all too apparent.

"The light doesn't seem to get any closer," Eugenia commented. "The longer we walk, the farther away it seems to be."

Grahame's heart dropped. She was correct. He had just come to the same conclusion. He stopped and looked around. It was now almost nightfall. They had less than a half hour left of twilight. The weather was not improving. They and the horses were tired, cold, and hungry.

There were times he couldn't see ten feet in front of him and others when he could barely see the elusive light. He would have to do something and do it fast. He had placed them in dire jeopardy, and he silently berated his foolishness. His leg ached terribly, and he knew he could not walk many more miles.

"Look! There's a cottage over on the edge of the woods," Eugenia called, and pointed to his right.

Grahame turned his steps in that direction. He could just make out the crofter's cottage, and a rush of relief filled his being. Damn, he could have cost them their lives, and he was horrified at his actions. He had been a soldier of the Empire and was trained to lead men into battle. He had court-martialed men for less negligence.

Eugenia struggled with her soggy skirts as they trudged slowly toward the cottage. "There is no light. Do you suppose it is empty?"

Grahame did not answer. The situation was not improving. They might save themselves from freezing in the snow, but for what? The implication of the circumstance he refused to entertain, putting it out of his mind with a shudder.

Eugenia's thoughts had not drifted along those lines yet. She was too cold and miserable to worry about being in an empty cottage with a man she hardly knew. That was the last thing on her mind. In fact, it had not yet occurred to her. She just wanted to be warm.

Three

The deserted crofter's cottage sat on a knoll, nestled among a stand of birch trees. While not dilapidated, it was neglected and abandoned in appearance. The whirling gusts of snow among the trees revealed the house like some mystical truth partially seen one minute and obscured the next. An ominous feeling grew with each step they took. The cottage seemed to wait in dark silence. Their steps at first had been eager, but now Lord Grahame and his ward approached with slowing stride and growing dismay.

"I am not sure if we can stay here," Lord Grahame said, his voice wary and subdued as he gazed at the dark, empty cottage.

"Well, I am! I cannot go another step farther." Eugenia stood next to him and looked up into his scowling face. "Frankly, at this moment it looks like a palace. Surely there is a fireplace, and that is all I can think about!"

"Yes, yes, of course," he answered, looking down at the forlorn creature at his side. "There is a barn on the other side for the horses, so it seems our only choice."

Eugenia tugged at the robe against the shiver that traveled the length of her body. The relief of his words brought a sting of tears beyond the cold to her eyes. She nodded and waited.

Grahame tied the lead horse to the fence and moved to the front door of the cottage. With the considerable force of his broad shoulders he thrust open the door. Eugenia stood shivering and watching with the concern of a condemned woman about to be pardoned. A broad smile burst forth the minute the door gave way. Scurrying to catch up to him, she ignored the lanterns, which by now were cutting into her arms and smashing against her thighs.

As the earl stepped inside, the waning daylight sent pale streams into the dim room. The light was enough to make out shapes so he took Eugenia's arm and entered the shadowy, frigid room. They stood side by side united momentarily by the cold reception of the room and the helpless feeling of the situation.

"Miss Dudley, I must first get the horses into that barn before they freeze and where I hope there is some fodder. I'll see about some firewood and return immediately." He set the hamper down. "We shall be grateful for this," he mumbled, then lit the lanterns Eugenia had carried and placed one on the mantel.

"You'll be all right until I return?" he asked.

"Of course, I shall look around and see what is here."

Lord Grahame, doubtful that little if anything had been left in the cottage, stepped outside and closed the door behind him.

Eugenia stood silently, looking around the sparse room. Realizing she was absolutely miserable with her wet skirts clinging to her legs, she stamped her feet and began to peruse the room. Something had to be done! There was a broken chair and a kettle hung in the hearth, all covered with dust. Dry leaves lay in the corners, and the signs where mice or squirrels had made their home were evident. She grimaced, hoping it was squirrels, a hope too optimistic to be true. She hated mice, but what were a few mice held against the prospect of freezing to death?

Lifting the lid of the woodbox, she found a supply of dry kindling. Her heart leapt at that good fortune. First she gathered the dry leaves and carried them to the hearth. Next she placed the kindling on top. With stiff fingers and quick movements she took a strip of wood and held it to the lantern flame. The sliver of kindling ignited into a little flicker that she carefully shielded as she slowly moved it to the hearth. In moments the little pile of wood came alive with a tenuous, flickering flame. She knelt before the fire, stretching her cold, stiff fingers to the welcoming warmth.

Well, she thought, I must get on. Reluctantly, she rose from the meager fire and removed the kettle left hanging on the hook. Pulling the lap robe around her, she braced herself against the onrush of cold air and opened the door. She piled snow into the kettle and winced with pain from her frozen fingers. Rushing back into the cottage, she hung the kettle over the fire and stood watching as the snow began to melt. Just the thought of some hot water sent warmth through her body.

The door flew open and banged against the wall as the earl entered with swirling snow and an armful of wood.

"You wasted no time, I see," he said, and smiled with pure admiration shining from his eyes.

Eugenia's eyes widened, for the transformation was remarkable. He was truly pleasing in appearance, and she realized he wasn't really very old. She stared in disbelief.

"Is something wrong?" he asked as he shoved the door closed the same way he had opened it—with his booted foot.

"No."

"Then why are you staring?"

"You smiled."

"Smiled?"

"Yes, it is the first time. It surprised me."

He returned her gaze in utter amazement. Never had anyone dared to discuss his expression, let alone a slip of a girl. "I was not aware my expression was your concern."

Eugenia wanted to strike him. The pompous ass! "Rest assured, my lord, it is of no consequence whether you smile or not. Since it seems to be a point of considerable contention for you, I must be correct in assuming it is not something with which you often deal!"

Now it was Lord Grahame's turn to wish to lay a cuff on the impudent chit. His eyes flashed anger, but he managed a shrug and stepped past her.

The situation was taking its toll on their dispositions. He had often found that to be the case with his men, and so he ignored the exchange.

Kneeling down before the little fire, he placed some logs on top and they immediately flared up in promising, lapping flames. He rose, rubbing his hands together over the glowing fire.

Watching his silhouetted profile, Eugenia realized he was most attractive—in a strongly masculine way. The thought was not comforting, and she stepped back, feeling suddenly defenseless.

Instantly, he sensed her anxiety and turned to look upon her face. The firelight played against the strong planes of his face and he appeared even more formidable. They stared at each other for several seconds.

"You have nothing to fear from me. I apologize for this misadventure, for getting us into this . . . er . . . predicament. But there it is, and nothing I can do will change the situation. Therefore, I suggest we make the best of it. You are not in danger of being ravished, if that is what brings the wide-eyed look of terror to your face."

"I am not so stupid as to suppose you would harbor nefarious designs on me. After all, I am your ward," she said, gathering all the hauteur she could muster, which was little enough. Eugenia had not seen hauteur of aristocratic proportions, and so her effort appeared a bit comic.

Grahame smiled and his eyes danced.

Eugenia stared at him. He was laughing at her!

"Credit me with more intellect than that! I fear, however, the danger may be yours," she said with a sway she had learned from the cook at the school who used it as an expression to subdue anyone who dared traverse into her domain.

How common she is, he thought, and smiled even more. Blanche has a worthy task, and at this moment it does not look promising.

"Will not the situation be compromising? Since I am your ward, that makes a very difficult predicament for you, I dare say." Her smile was smug as if to say "so there."

He laughed. He threw back his head and laughed loudly.

At this point Eugenia was certain she was in the presence of a madman. "You mean that does not frighten you?" she whispered incredulously.

"Frighten me? Heavens no! What do I care what some self-appointed arbiter of the ton thinks? I am merely carrying out the duty promised by my father. No less and no more, that is all that is necessary."

"What will your wife think?"

"I am blessed to have no wife. Now your curiosity is satisfied . . . I am unmarried." He offered a slight bow and infuriating smirk.

Eugenia dropped her gaze in embarrassment. He had guessed correctly; she was curious and wished to know. Anyone would be, she thought, but uttered a contrite "So it would seem, my lord."

"Good, we understand each other, then. Let us get on with whatever it is to best survive this night."

He took off his greatcoat and handed it to her. "Take this to cover yourself, but first remove your wet clothing. You'll die of the fever before morning if we do not get you out of those wet garments."

She took the heavy coat with a pounding pulse in her temples and a shaky hand. Take off her clothes? Great heavens . . . where? She looked around the one room cottage and shivered.

"I shall turn my back. You disrobe and put on my coat. It will not take long to dry out your garments. And you must agree that the coat will cover all that your maidenly modesty requires."

She was certain he was being sarcastic, and it rankled her. What else was there to do? She had to get out of the clothes, for she was chilled to the bone. Lord Grahame turned his back to her and said, "Proceed."

Eugenia obeyed with stiff, fumbling fingers. The lapsed time seemed an eon, but she finally managed to remove her garments. They dropped in a soggy pile around her feet. She stepped out of them and shifted into the capped greatcoat that hung to the floor and draped into a pool around her feet. It weighed a hundred stone at least, she thought in exaggeration. It was warm from his body heat, and she tingled with the comfort of the satin lining against her bare skin. She blushed at the sinful enjoyment of this sensual feeling.

"Are you finished yet?" he asked impatiently.

"Yes." Eugenia stood clutching the coat around her slender frame, looking woefully overwhelmed.

Lord Grahame turned and took pity on his bedraggled ward. "Do not worry. We'll see ourselves out of this all right and tight." He forced a positive-looking smile which failed in its mission, but Eugenia was glad for the offered sentiment and returned the smile.

"Here, no need to clutch the coat," he said, as he reached over and proceeded to button each button. Eugenia stood immobilized by those slender fingers as they moved along the coat—so close to her body.

"There, that is better. You can move about without worry," he said with a decided twinkle in his eye.

Eugenia did not answer. She stooped to gather up her clothes and began to shake them. She blushed with the realization that her undergarments were sadly mended, a dozen times at least.

Silent and red-faced, she strung them over the broken chair set before the fireplace.

When she had finished, she raised her eyes to his. "What now, my lord?"

He looked at this waif and wondered himself. What next? He could not show his uneasiness, for he did not want her frightened any more than she already was. He answered with a booming authority. Eugenia jumped.

"I will get some straw. We can't sleep on this cold floor. You see what's in the hamper, but remember that any food must last until tomorrow." He picked up the fur robe. He knew it would hold far more straw than his arms, and he wanted to make only one more trip into the cold night air. He folded the blanket with a grimace while considering it was the only one they had. It was going to be a long night.

Four

With creeping apprehension Eugenia watched the snowflakes that had blown in the open doorway. The dreadful fact was they remained where they fell. They did not melt! No wonder her feet felt like ice against the dirt floor. Quickly, she moved back to the fireplace, sat, and stuck her toes toward the fire, wiggling them in the warmth. The heat felt good, but now her bottom was freezing. The priory was always chilly, but never this bone-chilling cold.

She reached and wrung out her stockings again in order to hasten their drying, then replaced them back on the three-legged chair. She wondered if the chair would end as wood for the fire during the night. She supposed so.

Finishing her token effort to "do something," she drew up her knees and rested her chin on them. Weariness racked her body and joined cold as her companion. A hunger pang rumbled in her stomach. She smiled wearily; there was no end to her body's complaints.

Next, she reached for the hamper and opened the lid to the mingled aromas that drifted up, and she decided heaven must smell like apples and cheese. The delicious fragrances blended, sending hope and a rumble in her stomach that could probably be heard in London.

"What marvelous luck," she squealed, realizing they had a miracle. God bless Mrs. Henley and God bless Lila or so Lord Grahame had called his far-sighted servants.

They might freeze to death, but they would do so on full stomachs. The sardonic thought brought a wry smile to Eugenia's lips.

She was still smiling when she answered Lord Grahame's kick at the door. His arms were full of musty-smelling straw, and he carried an enormous bundle in the carriage robe. Moving past her, he dumped it on the floor in front of the fireplace. "This is our bed."

Eugenia stared in silence. There seemed no appropriate response. She stood mesmerized, watching Lord Grahame spread the straw. She knew she should help, but stood as charmed as a cobra by his movements. His signet ring flashed ruby fire with his strong, quick movements. It was so incongruous, a lord of the realm on his hands and knees spreading straw. The firelight played against the contours of his face and ruffled hair, and he was plainly pleasing to her eye. She would do well to put that thought out of her mind, for it was a very uncomfortable one. "It is difficult to think of an earl making a bed of straw."

He rose and glanced at her. "There have been times in my life that such accommodations would have been a great boon. You forget my life has been the life of military service, and not lavender-scented sheets."

Next, he flipped out the robe and spread it across

the straw. Eugenia reached down and evened the opposite ends.

"I'm starved. What wonders did Lila put in the hamper?"

His words brought her back to the moment, and she hurried to bring the basket to him. "A feast fit for an earl, my lord."

"Shall we dine?" he asked with an expansive wave of his hand as if he were addressing an assembly of dinner guests.

"I should be delighted, your lordship," she said with a wee curtsy as acknowledgment to his humor, then dropped beside him, tucking her bare feet under the coat.

"Ah, that feels good. Warmth and food, who could require more?"

"Amazing how quickly one can get to the essentials," he replied.

She nodded, but then, she had always known that.

"What has Lila sent along at the insistence of Mrs. Henley? We shall be indebted to my officious housekeeper. She is a lion at the gate, and I usually resist her motherly dictates, but from this moment forward I shall be a lamb to her bossy orders." He chuckled, and crinkles radiated from his eyes in the face that had spent many years in the open.

Eugenia smiled appreciatively at his obvious efforts to lighten the situation. For the first time, the prospect of his being her guardian took on an encouraging aspect.

"First, a bit of wine to warm us," he said, passing the uncorked bottle to her.

Gingerly, she raised it to her lips. The sweet liquid tingled her tongue and left a trail of warmth down her throat. The warmth spread through her body and limbs as she handed back the bottle. Lord Grahame took a deep gulp.

"Hmm, bread, cheese, and meat pies," he said, handing her a little pie wrapped in a linen serviette.

The rich aroma of meat and onions were a pale omen to the wonderful flaky crust and rich ingredients that filled her mouth. "Delicious," she said with a mouth full of crust, and gravy trailing from the corners. She closed her eyes—never had she been so hungry—not even at school. She opened her eyes to find Lord Grahame watching her. She blushed.

"Miss Dudley, I am profoundly sorry about our predicament."

"I know."

He was sure she did not, but he appreciated her kind tone. "We have to think about surviving the night. Perhaps we can keep the fact of our aloneness a secret. I'm not sure and I regret the implications. But a small scandal is infinitely more appealing than freezing to death."

Her mouth twitched. Her luminous eyes rested on him with candor. He saw no fear in them. Thank God, he thought, I do not have a missish female wailing doom on my hands. He ran his hand through his hair, wondering how to broach the next subject.

"I have pledged your safety with me," he said. "You have nothing to fear. You are my ward, and no harm will come to you under my care."

"You are trying to say we shall have to huddle together to stay alive?" she asked.

He stiffened in surprise. "Well . . . yes . . . I just

had not thought to place my words in that manner." While her blunt words annoyed him, he found himself grateful for her precise appraisal of his meaning and her lack of hysterics.

"You can dress up any situation into fancy words, my lord, but it is my experience: a fact is a fact."

"Of course, it is just that . . ."

"I am unmarried, homely, and you're obligated to find me a husband. With a reputation of having been compromised by spending the night with you only makes a difficult task impossible."

Lord Grahame was horrified. How explicit she was! That will never do when he introduced her to society. The future prospects dimmed even more, if that were possible.

"You are not making this easier by speaking so plainly," he replied, and his tone carried his disapproval.

"I disagree. I am making it very easy for you. I don't fear you, Lord Grahame. I believe you. The situation nor the company lends itself to seduction."

Again he was taken aback. By "company" did she mean he or she was without attraction? The idea brought a great amusement and his smile reached his eyes.

Eugenia dropped her eyes to hide a hammering heart. Her bravado hid her fear, but to her ears her well-chosen words held a hollow ring. Bravado had been her armor at school, but now, she realized, it had placed her at a disadvantage. She swallowed hard.

They finished the pies in silence. He offered another drink of wine before he corked the bottle and put it away.

"We'll save the rest for tomorrow. It may take Ben some time to find us. After all, we did not make the Boar's Head Inn."

"I am glad," she said without thinking.

"How so?" he asked, leaning back on his elbow and gazing at the fire.

"Well, it would have been embarrassing."

He turned to look at her. Eugenia felt another disquieting lurch in her chest. His eyes were so direct. They seemed to bore right through her, and she did not like it, much less her reaction to him.

"You are not embarrassed here?"

"Well, of course I am. But I believe what you told me, and there aren't others looking at us."

He arched an eyebrow. "You do not like people to look at you? Most women I know spend hours for just such a reaction."

"People usually never even notice me, so I never worry about it much. I do know I should not like it one bit if they did. Wouldn't it annoy you to have people speculating about you?"

"Frankly, I have never considered the matter. It has never occurred to me whether anyone was looking at me or not. From the opposite end of a gun barrel it might disconcert me somewhat," he said in jest. "How odd that it should concern you."

"Then, my lord, you have never been subject to the whims of others, or you would be well aware of their interest, approval, or whatever." She had wanted to add disapproval, but knew that was far too revealing. She turned her gaze from him.

Lord Grahame considered her words and did not comment on them. They continued to sit in silence. The room was dim and cold. Their breath hung in tiny crystal wisps. The fire offered some warmth, but not far into the room. Eugenia sat with her chin resting on her knees, still draped in the earl's coat.

Grahame studied his ward. She looked pitiful, as if the entire world rested on her slender shoulders. Perhaps it did.

"Durate, et vosbet rebus servants secundis," he muttered softly to himself.

Eugenia's eyes narrowed. "You're right, we will endure and live for a happier day," she said, and smiled.

"You know Virgil?"

"I have studied him," she replied primly.

He had no reply, for his ward seemed to offer a surprise at every turn.

The room grew colder. "See if some of your clothes are dry," he ordered.

His command startled her reverie and she jumped a foot. Quickly she obeyed, scampering to feel her undergarments. "Some are," she said.

"Good, get them on." He turned his back to her.

"Might I just sleep in the coat?"

"No, we will use that to sleep on and the fur rug to cover us."

"Us?"

"We'll barely survive the night with the warmth of our bodies, the fur rug, and the inadequate fire. Thank our lucky stars it's snowing so hard."

"How so?"

"It means it is not too cold when it snows this much."

Small comfort, Eugenia thought, watching Lord Grahame rise from the lap robe. It occurred to her that he must be very cold in only his jacket, and she felt guilty having sat snuggled in his coat with no thought of his comfort.

"I will close the inside shutters while you put on whatever is dry." He crossed the room to the window, never looking back.

She stepped out of the coat to the onslaught of cold air. Quickly, she struggled into her chemise. The hem was still damp and clung to her cold toes. She huddled in her arms. "I am ready."

He did not cast a look in her direction. She stood with a lump in her throat and watched as he spread out his coat, satin side up. Next, he furled out the fur rug. His shadow moved along the wall and ceiling. The fire caught his pale gray eyes and she could not tell if they held annoyance or amusement.

"Come, let us get some rest. I hope we can get leave tomorrow when Ben gets back with help."

Eugenia slowly dropped next to him. Gingerly, she stretched out, and he placed the fur rug over them.

"Hope? You hope we can leave? You mean you do not know if he will be back?" she asked in a thin, incredulous voice.

"Go to sleep, Miss Dudley. We shall take care of tomorrow—tomorrow."

Eugenia obeyed. Despite the appalling situation, she could not imagine being more tired than she was now. The emotions of leaving the only life she knew, the children, the trudge through the snow, and this terrible predicament rushed in. She wanted to cry. Her limbs felt heavy and her body so tired; it was beyond pain.

She closed her eyes, and the long length of Lord Grahame, stretched out under the covers next to her, was appalling. She was afraid she might accidentally touch him, but he kept his distance. They lay side by side with only inches, carefully observed, between them. This conscious effort held remarkable discomfiture for them both. Accompanying this awkward situation was the silence of their embarrassment, which made it worse.

She woke sometime in the night, when Grahame rose and left the makeshift bed. She could feel the cold air rush in where he had been. Keeping her eyes almost closed, she watched him put more wood on the fire and check the progress of the storm.

She heard him swear an oath. Oh, dear, she thought, it has not stopped snowing. She remained perfectly still.

He climbed back under the covers and drew her closer for warmth. She made no sound because his warmth was welcomed. She lay snuggled in his strong arms. A hot flush traveled her body when she realized they may be stranded in the snowstorm, but this was the first time she had felt truly safe since she was a girl. The impact was overwhelming and delicious. She savored the feeling and again fell asleep when she heard his even breathing.

Five

Eugenia stirred several times during the night, shifting whenever Grahame moved. The pervasive cold from the dirt floor seeped through the makeshift bed, reminding her of their whereabouts. Still, she remained reasonably warm from the fur cover and the proximity of their bodies.

At first it had been dreadfully embarrassing to lie so close, but later it became necessary for survival and any awkwardness faded. Abruptly placed into this intimate circumstance, unheard of in any social setting outside marriage or desire, they managed to accept it. In fact, the acceptance became a comfort when no other option was possible.

The circumstances allowed them to be themselves. One could hardly put on airs when all trappings of the salon were nonexistent and the intimacy of a bedroom surrounded them. Lord Grahame had easily accepted the situation, for it was a mere extension of hardships he had known in the army. Eugenia had never known the drawing room and the priory afforded little privacy and little comfort. She was able to accept the circumstances with tenacity. She was in no way offended, and for this Lord Grahame was ever grateful.

Grahame stirred and opened his eyes to a room

shrouded in semidarkness and flickering shadows. Embers glowed in the hearth, casting a soft glow into the dark room. Very carefully, so as not to disturb Miss Dudley, he rose from the stopgap bed, replacing the cover and moving to replenish the logs on the fire.

The room was deadly cold. He shivered. Adding the wood, he waited and watched the flames spring to life. Damn, it was freezing, he thought, and rubbed his hands by the fire. The cold floor sent icy shivers through his stocking-clad feet. He hoped tomorrow would bring their rescue, for he did not want to spend another night in this godforsaken place. He cast a glance to the sleeping Miss Dudley and marveled at her cool detachment. He doubted few ladies could have managed so awkward a situation without vapors. Blessings are found in unexpected places, he mused.

Next, he moved to the window to judge the condition of the outside world, and at that moment he felt as though he were "doing something." Opening the shutters, he could see only the gray light of dawn through the ice that had accumulated inside the window. He rubbed a spot clear and viewed a solely white world.

The air held that unique, eerie stillness that comes after a heavy snowfall. All sound was muffled, and the world lay in utter silence, making their isolation seem as though they were lost to the world. Grahame glanced once again to his sleeping ward, and a pang somewhere between pity and regret crossed his mind. I must get us out of here and soon, he thought. But he wondered about that possibility.

When he opened the door to five feet of snow

blown against the cottage, his frown deepened with growing apprehension. Good Lord, but they were in a mighty fix. They would not be easily found, and it would be equally difficult to leave.

One day missing might not be noted. We might get away with that, he thought, but more was bound to draw attention. I have to think of something. I will wait a while longer for Ben, but if he does not come soon, we will have to try to leave on the horses.

He piled snow into the pot and hung it on the hook for warm water. Creeping over to the bed, he slipped back under the cover. There was nothing else he could do, and it was the only warm place. He would have to feed the horses as soon as it was light, but he would need the coat they were sleeping on.

Eugenia, pretending to be asleep, watched the earl under veiled lashes and recognized apprehension from his drawn expression. Her heart skipped with a sliver of fear. "Is everything all right?" she asked as he settled in next to her.

His glance offered a deepening frown, which he quickly masked. "We are safe from freezing to death, and that is the most important factor now." He tried to put a light note in his voice, and Eugenia was grateful for his effort.

"Please do not worry. We will do just fine. You can send me to one of your estates, and no one need know we have been together all this time, alone," she volunteered.

"I am not worried. We will do well to escape with our lives, so all else fails in importance by comparison."

Eugenia did not reply, but smiled: He was correct. They continued to lie quietly side by side. The stillness was not awkward; it hung in resignation.

"What was school like?" Grahame asked, no longer sleepy and conscious enough of her shapely body to change his drifting thoughts with conversation.

Eugenia mulled over the question with summary thoughts, trying to assemble an idea of her recent past. "I have nothing to compare. I recall little of my life before being sent to the school. I know my life was happy, and I remember my mother. She was beautiful and laughed often, or at least I think she did, for I remember her laughter. The memories of my father are dimmer. I think of him as a giant in a scarlet coat. He was not home often."

"How old were you when my father took you there?"

"Eight. I never met your father. A gentleman in a black frock coat took me there. I was terrified. I was so alone, but I soon found to be alone can be a safe . . . *bon succor* . . . if you will."

"I know what you mean. Just before one goes into battle with thousands of men, there is a moment when one is all alone. I believe that is the only way one faces death."

"Or fate," she added.

They fell into a thoughtful silence. A log split and crashed in the hearth, sending a shower of sparks and flaring light. A sense of camaraderie became a shared experience, and it was comforting. Too comforting, thought Grahame, and he sat up.

"I must feed the horses. We will have to find a snowdrift and pretend it is an elegant privy, although it will be better than some I have experienced," he said, and chuckled. He was amazed at his lack of proper manners by addressing what is never spoken of and feeling not the least ill at ease. She did not make him feel the least uncomfortable.

He rose and offered his hand to her. "Wrap the carriage robe around you, for I need the coat. When we return we shall have a bit to eat."

Eugenia obeyed.

After attending the horses and reentering the cottage, it seemed warm and welcoming. What moments before had seemed like a horrible place to be now offered a homey greeting.

"It is almost cheery in here," Eugenia said.

"I agree. I was considering taking the horses and trying to make it out on our own. I think that might be foolhardy."

"You would have to tie me to a horse. I am frightened to death of them. They are so big!"

"You don't ride?"

"When would I have ridden?"

"What did you do?"

"I taught the children."

"You never had time for leisure or pleasure?"

"Well, the children were my pleasure and reading my escape."

"Hmm . . . it does not sound like much pleasure to me," he said, spreading the coat out again.

"When you have books you can learn anything in the world by reading, truly anything."

Lord Grahame chuckled. "It is my training that most things are learned by experience. In fact, there are some things that can be learned only by experience."

"Such as?"

Lord Grahame merely chuckled again. The laugh was such that Eugenia blushed. He was being devilish just to annoy her, but she could not help but smile. She liked the ease in which he placed them. It would have been a horrible experience with someone who was a high stickler or one with lascivious designs. She knew that was foolish, for she held it quite unlikely she would ever bring out the beast in a man. It was a comfort to understand that. Her smile broadened, for her mind had recently traveled where it had never gone before. At least this is diverting, she thought.

"Here," she said, opening the hamper and handing the wine bottle to him. She foraged for the cheese and bread. "A feast fit for a king, or, at least, an earl!"

Grahame watched her busy herself with breaking the bread. She is a strange little creature, he thought. Not nearly as unattractive as he had first thought. Those eyes were magnificent, and one could get lost in them. They seemed to dominate the space between herself and the person with whom she spoke. It was hard to tell about her hair, she braided it so severely. Wisps now escaped a heretofore perfect coiffure, and those strands seemed to shine hints of honey. There was an elegance in her movement almost as if she were a dancer. She held her head with the same elegant pride. It was natural, for he knew she had had no training. It gave her considerable allure. He tore his gaze away when her eyes met his, wondering if she read his thoughts.

Eugenia handed him a piece of cheese and bread, which he accepted with a nod and smile. He did not look so formidable sprawled out on a crofter's cottage floor. Still, he did look noble; she supposed he always would.

There was a sense of command about his person,

and she was sure it was his military training. While she did not think him kind, he did show concern. Naturally, it was his life as well as hers that concerned him, and well it should. She knew they would be found. It was *survival* that frightened her. She would have to go away somewhere or the scandal would ruin him.

"What terrible thoughts crowd your mind? You look so serious," he asked.

"To be perfectly honest, I was wondering where I should go when we are rescued. You do not deserve a scandal."

The thought took him by surprise. He had previously denied that fact to her. He had continually put the notion from his mind with the immediacy of events. He rolled on his back, put his hands behind his head, and stared at the blackened ceiling.

"We shall worry about that in time. There is nothing we could have done unless we continued with Ben. Then we would not have had to concern ourselves about the circumstances, for you would have died of the lung fever."

Eugenia beamed with an idea. "That is it! The very thing! I could have become frightfully ill and not been able to continue the journey. You gallantly took care of me. And no gentleman would take advantage of a dying ward."

"I am a gentleman?"

"Of the highest order, I assure you."

Grahame turned his head and smiled. "Won't fly, a little indisposition would not thwart dalliance any more than it will thwart the tongues of the tabbies. You must not worry, please. I shall take care of it."

Eugenia nodded, but she felt terrible. It was his honor to take his father's obligations and it would be his honor called into question. It did not seem fair, but then, she knew more than most that "fair" was never an equitable condition.

"We'll wait a while longer for Ben. Stay warm and try to get some rest," he commanded. "We might just have to hoof it out of this mess. If Ben does not come, and I have the greatest faith he will, it will take considerable time to get to Windhaven. Either way will take all your stamina, so close your eyes and try to sleep."

Six

Lord Grahame prowled the room relentlessly. The helpless inactivity was difficult for a man accustomed to decision and action. Suddenly, he flopped down on the blanket next to Eugenia, who had been watching his growing restlessness with sympathy. He rubbed his aching leg and scowled.

"My lord, does your leg pain you?"

"My leg bothers me when the weather is damp and cold, and when I have been on it too long. When I am occupied, I do not notice the pain, but now I am bored beyond measure."

"Bored?"

"Yes, bored. You must be, too! I am about to go around the bend . . . stranded in this godforsaken place."

She stared at him. *Bored?* Never had she experienced a more exciting time! Was it that she was out of the dreadful school or that she was isolated in a cottage with *him?* The latter thought sent a shiver down her spine and a flush to her cheeks. She should dispense with that thought! He was attractive, yes. He was interesting, yes. He was for her, no. She twisted her fingers in a fidgety gesture.

The sudden pang of being a burden swept her. They had to get out of there before it was too late!

In her wildest dreams a man of Lord Grahame's station would always be above her touch. He is bored; nothing else need be said.

Searching for something to change her wayward thoughts, she asked, "What activities do you participate in that keep you from boredom? It has been my observation that if one has a mind, one need never be bored." She realized she sounded inflated.

"Really?" Lord Grahame asked, lifting an eyebrow. "How gratifying for you. Never to be bored, hmm."

"Well," she said, settling down with a knowing expression that immediately rankled Lord Grahame. "Whenever I was lonely I would just think of things that pleased me. For instance, once I saw a beautiful woman all dressed in silks. The lady looked as though she had never cried in her life, as if she had been protected always from any unpleasantness. She walked past me and smiled. She was like a summer garden. She moved as softly and as easily as a breeze. I think of her often."

"Why?" he asked, his interest peaked.

Eugenia blushed. "I heard her companion, who seemed to fairly dote on her, call her Jenny. Is not that the most charming of names? Jenny. It sounds so soft and feminine, and suited her perfectly."

"How fanciful you are. I should have thought the school would have denied you any whimsical thoughts."

"Ah, that is just my point. You must see that. When all else is darkness our minds can take us anywhere."

What an odd one she was, but then, he had seen the dismal priory. The image of a lonely child with imaginary dreams to carry her from her surroundings caused him to shift in disquietude. He could imagine her sitting by the pale light reading to escape, and he regretted her virtual abandonment. He hid his thoughts and continued on their conversation.

"Hmm . . . would you like to be such a lady?"

"Oh, I never could. One must be born to it, but every lady would delight in being akin to Jenny. Every gentleman wants a Jenny."

"How do you know what every man wants? You would be a Jenny to get a husband?"

"What an ugly thing to say. Of course not! I would be Jenny simply because it would be smashing! Think how deadly dull 'Eugenia Dudley' is. You must agree, the name is part of the myth."

"I am gratified to hear you say it is a myth, because it is. Jenny could easily be short for Eugenia. I think it would be appropriate."

"Oh, you do not see what I mean! Jenny is not just a name . . . it is a point of view. It comes from being pampered and never having met sadness or hardship."

"You do not believe anyone lives without sadness or hardship?"

Eugenia pondered his question. "Jenny does, without doubt."

"You are wrong. Everyone carries sorrow sometime. That is what all life is: overcoming our adversities."

"Well, I am certain one need not have them if one is lucky."

"Is that what *you* want?"

"Great heavens, I can never have that! I already know what life can be. Having seen battle, so must you."

"I am glad I hear no rancor in your words, for you are too young to be cynical. You speak of an earthly paradise that could not possibly exist. Besides, it would be deadly dull—to never have known opposition or adversity."

"Nevertheless, I should have liked to find out." Eugenia laughed at the silliness of their conversation. She noted Lord Grahame no longer rubbed his injured leg. He was interested in their conversation.

"I shall have to see that you become like Jenny." His smile crinkled his eyes, and he was no longer the aristocratic earl but a playful companion.

Eugenia clapped her hands. "By all means do," she teased in return, and rolled her eyes in feigned modesty.

"You think I am jesting?"

"Aren't you?"

"No."

Suddenly, she felt uncertain. She had disclosed too much. "Pay me no mind, my lord. It is just a ploy I played at school to while away dull hours."

Grahame sat with his arm on his knee and gazed into the fire. His duty to the girl suddenly took on a different aspect. She was now flesh and blood, a tangible person, not some obligation to be foisted off on someone else. The gravity of that commitment weighed upon him, and he shook his head. He must find the girl a suitable husband, one who would be kind. This child needed kindness. He turned and cast an appraising glance over her. With the right fixing up, she might just do.

They continued their conversation, speaking on a wide range of subjects, and he became impressed with the extent of her education.

"It is surprising that you acquired so wide an education from such a drab school."

Eugenia laughed. "Lest I sound too boastful, that was another of my gambits. Daydream or study. Since one has never learned anything new by listening to oneself, I found great pleasure in reading."

Grahame smiled. "Classics?"

"Yes."

"Latin, Greek?"

"Yes. I am sure my pronunciation is incorrect, but I could learn that soon enough."

"Indeed, I shall see to it."

"You would do that for me?"

"My father decreed it. It is my duty to do so. I am a soldier foremost, and duty is paramount. I regret my father neglected you so. We can make allowances for the poor health of his later years. I suppose Mr. Harrison, his man of business, took care of the details and Father never gave it another thought."

"I sound a sorry burden. How awful to be an obligation and even worse for you."

"I have learned from what you have told me, you believe that some things must be accepted. If you obey me, we shall see you settled very well indeed."

"I will have some say in the matter?" she asked with creeping apprehension.

"Of course. I cannot imagine marrying where one did not wish. That would be the ultimate unhappiness."

She stared at him. "I agree." The sadness in her voice was surprising, for it seemed unwarranted. Eugenia could not have given a reason to it, but there it was. She felt some vague pang of regret.

"I advise adding *Vita, noli me tangere* to your coat of arms," he teased.

"That is surprising. I should have thought you would chose *Knowledge and Armed.*" She leveled her striking eyes to his in the same candid probe she had given him when first they met.

The impact of her gaze sent the same quake through his body. It was astonishing and disconcerting. How odd, he thought, and his immediate impulse was to escape.

"We can't wait a minute longer. We have whiled away enough time," Grahame announced, and swiftly rose to his feet. "We must make our own way out of here. Ben does not know where we are, and there is no telling how long it will take him to find us. There can be no tracks left after that storm."

Eugenia nodded in agreement, wondering if that meant she would have to ride.

"Will I have to sit on a horse?"

"Unless you prefer to remain behind. I could come for you later," he said, waiting for the effect of his words.

Eugenia glanced around the room with a shudder. It was one thing to be with the earl and quite another to be here all alone.

"Oh, no, no, I will manage quite well," she said, shaking out the blanket in preparation to leave. If only she could believe her own words.

It was a long wait before Lord Grahame walked the harnessed team to the front of the cottage. The sky was still rolling in gray clouds, but it was no longer snowing. They had a chance. If they did not reach Windhaven, they would, in all likelihood, find an inn.

Eugenia moved out to meet him. She stood and waited instructions while clutching her cape and the lap robe as Grahame brought up the huge, snorting creatures. She shrunk back as their breaths sent out billowing clouds and reminded her of great beasts from some Celtic tale.

Grahame threw the blanket over the lead horse. Putting out his hand to Eugenia, she moved slowly forward to take it. He put his hands firmly on her waist, lifted her up, and placed her on the back of the monster.

"You can open your eyes, Miss Dudley. You are quite safe, I assure you," he said, swinging up behind her.

He took the rein in his right hand, then placed his left arm around her firmly. He pulled her close and wrapped the skirt of his coat across her lap.

"Do you feel safe?"

She did and nodded. The strength of his arm and hard-muscled chest made her feel as firmly secured as a planted oak. The warmth of his body seeped through her clothing, and she wondered just how safe her heart was. She debated whether the height of the horse or his nearness was causing the light-headedness that engulfed her.

They started forward through the deep snow, and she held her breath. The security of Grahame's arm and the obvious ease with which he sat the horse soon took hold, and she felt her body relax. She leaned into him and sighed.

"That is better, Miss Dudley. You see it is not so difficult after all." His words caressed her.

The wind had deposited the snow in uneven drifts, thus making it necessary to seek the terrain where it had not blown deep. The trek was arduous, and it seemed forever before they came to the main road.

"We walked farther than I thought. It would have taken Ben three days to find us." He shifted, searching to see if he could find his disabled coach. It was nowhere in sight; buried under the snow, no doubt.

They rode out onto the main road. Misgivings wrinkled Lord Grahame's brow; it was going to be a struggle to keep on track. He kneed the sides of the horse to pick up speed and the team began to move in unison. He must make haste, for they had miles to go.

For the first time since the misadventure began, Grahame knew his decision to stay overnight in the cottage had been sound. Miss Dudley could not have withstood last evening's buffeting storm. Now she was warm and rested. They had a chance.

A world covered with snow as thick and fluffy as cream lay before them. Tree limbs hung heavy, weighted with the clouds of white. The silence was broken only by the trudging hooves and snorting horses.

The air was crisp and cold. It invigorated the mind. Not a living soul was to be seen. They were the only two survivors in their white world.

"We're fortunate the storm subsided. I hope Ben managed to make Windhaven. If anyone could, it would be him. He is a fine horseman, and I rest easy knowing he is on his way back to us."

Eugenia could not utter a word. She was too high and he too close. She nodded feebly and squeezed her eyes tight for a second. He aroused emotions that were foreign. She must not allow this man to affect her. She straightened her back and a sliver of cold air slipped between them. He tightened his arm and pulled her back against him.

"I need your warmth, Miss Dudley."

So do I, she thought, and may heaven help me. She was conscious of his face so close to hers. His every movement, his nearness and breath on her cheek, came into her awareness with clear, precise detail. To her horror, she knew she waited for each movement and the next sensation with growing attention.

They continued along the lonely road to Windhaven. Eugenia became lost in a world of warm new feelings. She rested, lulled by the cadence of the horse, Grahame's warm body and the beat of his heart. Abruptly, she felt him tense, and her mind snapped back to reality. The delicious languor disappeared. She straightened, but his arm tightened and he held her firmly.

"I think it is Ben," he said, pointing to a black speck on the horizon.

They peered as the moving figure drew nearer. Grahame waved with enthusiastic relief and a hug for Miss Dudley. Ben waved his hat in recognition and shouted across the expanse.

"It seems we have been rescued," Grahame said with a whisper in her ear.

I wonder from what, she thought.

The new world that awaited Eugenia Dudley was beyond her vivid imagination. She had existed in the isolated world and strict routine of the Addington School for Young Ladies. The easy, intimate relationship and open conversations with the earl were not found and certainly not considered proper in the society she was about to enter. The society valued birth station and deportment above all else, and judged a young lady on her entrances, her carriage, her voice, and ability to allude an aura of flawless propriety.

Seven

"Good morning, Miss Dudley," the maid said, dropping a curtsy, then proceeding to cross the room to replenish the fire. The embers sprang to life, sending a glow throughout the room. The maid continued with her early duty and next opened the draperies to the weak morning sun. Eugenia stretched but remained cozily tucked beneath the covers, for the room held an early morning chill and the bed was so inviting.

"Your breakfast will be sent up in a moment. Lady Sinclair has requested you remain in bed and rest." The maid gazed at Eugenia with speculative interest, again curtsied, and left the room, closing the door ever so quietly.

Eugenia marveled at Grahame's obvious high stock on silently closing doors. She had noticed it the previous evening and it was still true, the servants tippy-toed about with nary a slam of a door.

The memory of the children and their boisterous exits brought a smile that faded into a parade of fine lines across her forehead. The children—it was the first time she had thought of them! The luxury of her new surroundings was already dulling the edge of that reality. Shocked by this realization, she silently vowed to do something about them if ever she could.

Snuggling into the satin-covered eiderdown, she forced aside the poignant thought and began to survey the room in which she was resting. The room was gorgeous. Never had she seen anything to compare. It was huge. The walls above the wainscot were pale mauve damask. Window draperies and bed dressings were of the same fabric trimmed in heavy gold fringe. In places where sunlight streamed in, the fabric had faded into softly graying tones. This did not detract from the elegance of the room, which was enhanced by a timeless quality. The wainscot and bed were heavily carved with garlands and cherubs. The ceiling was high and corbeled with carved cross-members.

The room conveyed wealth and comfort combined with stability and offered her her first real sense of security. She marveled at the idea and nestled deeper into the softness of the counterpane. She could stay there forever.

The room, despite its elegance, did not intimidate her. The earl did. True, he had been nothing but kindness and understanding when they were stranded, but she knew very well that he had tried to conceal his dismay.

What in heaven's name was going to happen to her—to them, for that matter? The predicament could not be worse, and yet her new life boded to be better than anything she had previously known. She knew she should feel more guilt about Lord Grahame, but to be out of that terrible cold and dark place was heaven.

Still, she worried. It was difficult to remain unflappable to an unknown future. "Silly," she reminded herself. "All futures are unknown." Saying that aloud did not ease her anxiety, and she bolted up in the luxurious bed.

Luxury could be a trap! Security could, too! You might give up everything to have one or both. She assumed people did so all the time. How much would she be willing to give up for security, for warmth and time to spend among books? To be able to join with others who appreciated such endeavors, and the known answer hovered menacingly. She buried her face in her hands and trembled with doubt. Would she sell herself into some arranged marriage for it?

Her uncomfortable thoughts were interrupted by the entrance of two maids. One carried an elaborate tray; the other was there as an assistant. They placed the bed tray, which held a silver vase of lily of the valleys and was draped in starched linen, on the bed. With a flourish a maid lifted the silver cover.

Eugenia's appetite roared with approval. Eggs, kippers, toast and thick slices of ham met her delighted eyes. The succulent aromas reached her nostrils, and she sighed.

"It smells wonderful," she exclaimed.

"His lordship likes a good table, he does," the youngest maid said while the other nodded approval. "May we fetch you anything else?"

"Heavens no. I could not imagine more!"

"Just ring if there is anything you might wish."

"Ring?" Eugenia asked.

The maids glanced at each other. "Yes, just pull this bell-pull and someone will come to answer whatever you wish."

Eugenia nodded, wide-eyed. "Yes, thank you."

The two maids curtsied and left—softly closing the door.

Eugenia watched the closed door a moment, then glanced back to the bell-pull. There was so much to learn. Before she could put into thought her lack of experience in what was commonplace to these people, her stomach growled. Realizing she was ravenous, and since no one was there to witness, she ate with a relish not fit for company.

Providence had been with them in the turn of good weather. Thank goodness they had decided to leave when they did. She closed her eyes to the possibility of lasting much longer in that cold cottage with no food.

Just then the door opened and in floated a stylishly dressed lady. She was young and attractive, older than Eugenia by only a few years. Her carriage was erect and her confidence obvious. She wore a dress of white muslin with a rose spencer. Her dark hair was arranged in curls, which framed an oval face of serene beauty. A pair of silver-gray eyes shone in kindness, and while they were the same color as the earl's, they carried none of the flint steel of his lordship's. She carried a Kashmir shawl tucked around her shoulders. Eugenia knew it was Blanche, under whose auspices she would fall.

"I am Lady Sinclair, the Earl of Grahame's sister. You must call me Blanche. After all, we are going to be the best of friends," she said, and pulled up a chair. "Are you feeling quite the thing this morning? What a dreadful experience . . . I am so sorry."

"I am fine, just a little tired, that is all." Eugenia's voice carried a wispy quality she had not intended.

"Well, I should have been quite devastated by such an experience. You must be given credit for your bravery. Thomas has mentioned it with great admiration, I assure you."

Eugenia blushed at her high praise.

"We are delighted to find you so well. We will see you rested, but then there are a million and one things to do." Blanche waved a slender hand fairly dripping in diamonds.

Eugenia watched the cultivated lady with fascination. She carried an air of self-assurance that could not be missed. Yet she was comfortable, for the woman seemed genuinely concerned.

"I beg your tolerance. We have much to do before the entire local gentry descend upon us to view the survivors of so fearsome a happening."

"You mean people know?"

"Unfortunately, they will."

"How?"

"Servants, my dear. They always know and are more than willing to pass it along. And believe me, they cannot compare to the gentry's love of gossip. So we must be prepared for the onslaught."

"Oh, my. I had hoped, I mean, I am worried about Lord Grahame," Eugenia said.

Blanche's gaze narrowed with interest. She could see genuine distress for Thomas, and it did not appear to be self-serving. That was an admirable sign, she decided.

Blanche examined the girl's features. She was no beauty, to be sure. However, her eyes were incomparable. If she chose pomona green, why, a person would never get past her eyes.

"Come, stand out of bed. Let me look at you. How tall are you?"

Eugenia obeyed and slipped from under the covers and stood before Lady Sinclair with more than a little embarrassment.

"I do not wish to make you uncomfortable, but we must get a start on some gowns. You will be under scrutiny as you have never been. We must do our best. My brother is insistent that we carry off this adventure as though nothing amiss has happened."

"I refuse to be a burden to Lord Grahame. He was wonderful. Really, I must not make a problem for him. Why cannot he just send me to one of his farms to live? I think I should love that above all else."

At first Blanche was shocked. A farm? Then she looked at the young lady with a decided gleam of approval. It was good to know she was not an adventuress. She shuddered to think how some ladies would seize this opportunity with the catch of the Season.

"Nonsense," Blanche responded with a wave of her hand. "You will do just fine. I have a feeling we can turn you out looking smart and smashing. I have always thought that to be smart looking is far superior. Do you not agree?"

Before Eugenia had a chance to agree or not, Blanche hurried on. "After all, the Lord gives us our looks. Anyone can be beautiful if they are born so. Ah, but it takes a clever woman to be stylish. I shall take stylish over beautiful any day of the year. It lasts longer than pretty, by the way." Blanche smiled and placed her hands on her lap.

A wry smile flitted across Eugenia's lips. It is easy for her to say; she is beautiful.

"Now, turn around, dear."

Eugenia blushed at this inspection. She curled her toes in discomfort against the rich silk Kashan carpet.

"You will do, but it will take some work. It cannot be done overnight. Please forgive my frankness in this matter. We will go to London to find the necessary clothes, and I shall not allow anyone but Henri to touch your hair. He will know precisely what to do. The style you are wearing may have been practical to manage and suitable for an orphanage, but it is too old and severe for your heart-shaped face."

"You are kind to offer help, but I do not need to be smashing."

"You most certainly do! After all, we will reflect on Thomas, and it behooves us to present ourselves in the best light possible."

"Thomas?"

"Lord Grahame, dear. You will reflect upon his consideration, and we owe it to him to look our best. Now, do not you agree?"

"Well, yes, of course. Put in that context, I could hardly disagree, but I have no money."

"Money? Why ever do you need money? Thomas will give us what we require. *My* heaven's, child, you *are* a worrywart. Imagine worrying about money! You will find Thomas, or Lord Grahame, generous to a fault!"

Eugenia stood staring at this lovely lady. Imagine worrying about money? Is she daft? Those words could be spoken only by one who *had* money. Suddenly, she felt as though she had walked into the middle of a play and was trying to catch up to the action. It was as if something were missing and certainly unknown. She did not want to risk looking even more foolish, so she stood and meekly nodded while Blanche walked around her, appraising her figure and touching her braids.

Blanche pulled the servant's bell and said, "Are you ready to begin?"

"I have a strong notion it would not matter, so I shall agree," Eugenia said, to what she was not sure, but she knew she was about to find out.

Blanche laughed. "You are so right, my dear. I like a quick mind. Good, we understand each other. We must put Thomas's welfare above all else."

In just moments the door again opened and a string of servants filed in carrying hot water and a bathing tub. One maid brought oils, soaps, and scents. Another carried towels, followed by maids carrying several dresses. A fat and flushed seamstress brought up the rear. When the footman had poured the hot water and departed, Blanche gave a nod to the seamstress.

Eugenia found herself being measured while various dresses were held up to her for an appraisal.

"I apologize for starting with hand-me-downs, but since all your clothes were 'stolen' from the carriage, we must make do until we can get to London. Blanche sent her a very speaking I-dare-you-to-contradict-me look.

Eugenia opened her mouth to speak.

"Never *mind*, dear, we will do fine. Do not say a word."

Eugenia got the message and obediently stood still while they discussed, measured, and settled on several solutions.

"We shall leave her hair until Henri can cut it. Ellen, see what you can do to soften it a little around her face."

Blanche's maid agreed, and the entourage set to the task like worker bees in a hive. Eugenia would not have been surprised if they had buzzed.

Blanche watched the proceedings, then turned to leave, the dressmaker in tow. "I shall call in later to see how all is progressing. Be a dear, and do not worry."

Eugenia nodded in hesitation. That was too tall an order. Yet she knew her words to be the truth. What could she do but turn herself over to the ministrations of this band of busy bees? Who knows what might come about? Eugenia smiled at the image of herself overdressed and still the waif in silk-masquerade. She pursed her lips and steeled herself. Let them do their worst, which would be an improvement.

Eight

Blanche entered her brother's study without so much as a knock. She strode in like a flagship of the line, a determined expression set firmly on her face. Lord Grahame looked up from his work and reluctantly replaced the quill. Sitting back in his chair, he made a thoughtful arch with his fingers against his lips. He was in for a lecture and resigned to it. Cleverly expecting such an overture, he had already set his answers to her probable demands. He remained watchful and wary as she prepared to broach *the* subject.

She took a chair and began. "Thomas, I am very concerned. It simply must not get out that you were stranded overnight, alone in an abandoned cottage! Her reputation will be ruined! I *wish* you had listened to me."

"So you have previously said—on several occasions. Frankly, I wish I had listened to you, too."

She ignored his sarcasm. "You should have allowed me to accompany you. I would have gladly come from Tower House."

"Blanche, I thought I would be back before nightfall. The weather turned impossible. Only divine intervention or inspiration could have changed that. I also thought I was fetching a child, not a young lady.

"It always amazes me how women lay claim to the unlikely fact that they could have dealt with an event more successfully, and then are only too eager to impart that information ever after."

Blanche lifted a delicate eyebrow. "Solely for the reason that it is probably correct."

Her brother scoffed.

"No one must know," she continued.

"Who would know?"

"Your coachman for one, and I should imagine every servant in your household."

"I shall make it understood: It is not to be repeated."

"How naive of you. I have never known servants, no matter how faithful, who did not discuss the happenings of the household. Thomas, it simply cannot become known. She could never survive a scandal. She does not have the position. She is well spoken and articulate, but she looks more a waif than a lady of quality. I despair for her."

"Her father was a man to be greatly admired. He was a brave soldier. My understanding is that her mother was beautiful and charming," Lord Grahame said.

"How could you know?"

"From the highest authority, I assure you. You would have thought some family member of hers would have taken an interest. Nevertheless, it was to Father that Major Dudley left the care of his only daughter. Poor care, that, by your description. A mark against us I mean to correct."

"Exactly my sentiments! You should offer for her.

It is your duty to do so. You brought her to this pass."

Grahame had been lounging back in his chair, but upon that expected but somehow startling announcement he shifted forward. His eyes narrowed. "Just what are you proposing?" His deep voice carried an ominous tenor and his icy eyes glittered menace.

"Thomas, do not try to frighten me with your fierce looks and 'major' demeanor. It will not qualify! I know you too well. The child is in a scrape because of you. She has little to offer, and it will be the devil to find her a husband."

"So I should be the sacrificial lamb?"

"You made the situation. She is your responsibility."

"You are a hard woman, Blanche."

"How unchivalrous of you to say so. What is to become of her? She has had little enough in life. And now hope of a proper marriage is quite lost."

"Blanche, not for one minute would you entertain a marriage with someone you barely knew and held no affection. Look how happy you are with Lloyd."

"I would not have managed to get myself in such a predicament. You owe the girl an offer of marriage. I have always considered you an honorable man, and it is your duty to offer for her."

"I cannot believe what I am hearing. Having spent my life in the service of my country, you now suggest I wed out of duty to society's hypocritical dictates. I will not do it. Money will buy her a husband."

"You have not shown any hurry to get a wife. The line needs securing, and you have not set foot in a ballroom—to the everlasting regret of a whole season of hopeful ladies."

Grahame scoffed. "No one would know whether I have entered the petticoat line or not."

"You foolish man! You cut quite a dash, even if you are not aware of it. Many hopeful ladies wait patiently for a nod from you."

"Blanche, you become more fanciful by the moment. I attract no attention, nor do I wish any."

"That is exactly my point! Since you are not about to get a wife, why not Eugenia? She would suit you. She is without silly notions of girls her age, which would drive you around the bend. She is not spoiled. And I strongly suspect she is what one might call 'capable.' That should suit you very well."

Thomas stared at his sister, knowing that in some corners of her triad she was correct. But why in hell should he sacrifice himself?

"I will think about it," he murmured.

"I should hope so. Now, please excuse me. There are a dozen details to attend. This whole debacle needs careful attention if we are to right this mess."

"I often wonder how I would ever get along without your guidance," he said with a derisive smile as she left the room.

"You could not manage this without me, I assure you," she said as she slipped through the door.

Lord Grahame laughed. She was probably right. He understood little of the foibles of his peers and cared even less. Think about it, he did. He sat staring into the fire long after Blanche's departure. He had long since given up any hope of accomplishing any work. He knew she meant well, and in some ways it was logical. Duty and honor were the creeds of the Winslows. In fact, it took prominent place on the family crest. Duty was one thing, but to marry for it, quite another.

How could he attach himself to this poor orphan? Yet that was the most convincing reason. She was an orphan, put into the care of his father by a man who had saved his father's life. Could he do less? He was a man of honor! How unfair life can be, he thought.

What if he were courting a lady now? That reasoning could not be used, for he was unattached. He had been so busy taking over his duties as the Earl of Grahame that he had lacked time to consider a wife. He knew he would marry eventually, but somehow he had assumed it would just come about. Grahame rubbed his temples. It was his duty to offer.

The earl found Eugenia in the library later that day. She looked scrubbed and fresh. The odd notion of shiny, crisp apples crossed his mind. He shook away the foolish image but continued to admire her gorgeous complexion. It glowed like ivory. She raised her glorious gold-green eyes and looked to him with a hovering fear. Good God, he thought, she is frightened to death. Poor child, she did not deserve all life had dealt her. Compassion, unfamiliar to his military training, gripped his mind.

The planned speech about finding her a suitable husband faded from his mind, and he heard himself utter words that came as a surprise to him.

"Miss Dudley, might I speak to you a moment?"

She continued to stare, her heart in her throat. His expression was so serious. My, but he is handsome to behold. There was not an inch of him that did not bespeak his masculinity. It was not classical symmetry of features but a way of moving and leveling his eyes that left one quite breathless. She smoothed the soft silk skirt, glad for her new gown. She felt elegant, for never had she owned so beautiful a gown. A tentative smile hovered with a nervous quiver.

"Of course, my lord."

"Miss Dudley, my sister had pointed out the difficult predicament in which we find ourselves. You are aware of it, for it concerned you when we were . . . er . . . lost. I feel it best that I offer marriage and therefore ask you to be my wife."

Fire flushed in Eugenia's cheeks, her heart leapt into a frantic cadence, and her mind buzzed. His words shook her. *Will you be my wife* tumbled over and over in her mind. Joy sprang in Eugenia, first in the throes of hero worship. How could it be otherwise? So handsome a man had rescued her from a life of mere existence. He showed nothing but kindness during their adventure, and now she sat in his home dressed in silk. She was not without the romantic notions of the young, and therefore she gazed on him with such adoration, Lord Grahame shifted with discomfort.

"I am concerned for you," he continued. "I should have thought you would like a Season with all the parties and pretty gowns."

She continued to stare, speechless. Did not he understand she knew nothing of that sort of life? Cared less? Finally, she mustered a whisper. "Those things mean nothing to me, my lord."

"Hmm, er, yes, of course." He ran his finger around his neckcloth.

He is uncomfortable, she thought. He is offering out of duty. For one silly second, she had entertained something quite different. "Lord Grahame, I can plainly see it is honor that prompts your kind offer. I cannot allow you to sacrifice yourself in some misguided sense of duty. I release you from all obligations by categorically refusing you. I do not wish to marry you."

The earl stood dumbfounded and completely taken aback. The fact that he was taken aback astonished him even more than her refusal. Why should her swift outright refusal rankle him? He wanted just such an answer. But she did it without a hint of hesitation. For a split second he was nonplussed, his confidence tweaked, his male ego pinched, and he marveled. Rejection was something he had never expected and he did not understand. Somehow he had wanted her approval—how odd.

He studied her a moment. The young lady sitting before him had possibilities and mettle. "I am convinced you will do very well, indeed. Since you will not have me, I shall provide for you, and you may marry where and when you wish, assuming he is suitable." Feeling magnanimous with this offer, and having discharged his obligation, he shrugged with a sigh of relief.

Miss Dudley offered a knowing smile. Charming to be sure, but too knowing for comfort. He excused himself and left the room with unflattering swiftness.

Eugenia struggled to withhold a scream that sat aggressively in her throat. The pompous ass! She knew better than he just how desirable she was as a prospective wife. Her chances for success in the marriage mart were next to nothing. Well, he said he would provide for her and probably would have to for the rest of her life, unless he was powerful enough to get her a husband.

The memory of the night in the cottage came to her mind. The image of his masculine form stretched out beside her on the rough bed of their making crowded unbidden to her mind. She felt a cold sense of loss and rebuked herself for the stupid thought. One could not lose what one never had. Still, she had the memory of their time together. It made no difference if she married or not. She was afraid her heart had been given to the first man she met.

Eugenia rose slowly and crossed the room, only to stare unseeingly out the window. She knew her life had been cheerless before, but now it mirrored the bleak winter garden. She had a glimpse of paradise and could never be content with earthly reality again. Abruptly, she smiled to herself. She was as smitten as any schoolgirl, and she could get over the affliction. Millions did.

Nine

Blanche was not placated by Thomas's promise of finding his ward a husband. For the time being she would accept his pledge, but doom seemed to hover, and she was sure they would eventually hear gossip. To circumvent that possibility, she decided to test the waters, as it were. Summoning Eugenia, Blanche requested that she ready herself for a visit with their neighbors, the Rankins. The family had lived in the vicinity for generations. In fact, their cousins had wed some generations back.

Assuming the country squire and his wife would reflect the common thought among the local gentry, she decided to pay a call. Blanche knew that their mustering past the local aristocracy did not necessarily mean they could do likewise among London's high sticklers. But, she reasoned, it was a means to see how the tale had spread and the response it generated. That would help to determine what necessary steps should be taken.

Blanche nodded approval to Miss Dudley when she presented herself, and they prepared to leave. The girl was not outstanding, but she was interesting. There was something appealing about her.

When they went to London she would see Eugenia dressed to the nines. It occurred to Blanche that they might well be in worse straits if Eugenia were an outstanding beauty. Jealousy has a way of coloring such decisions, and since the Rankins had a daughter they wished to fire off, she was momentarily glad Eugenia was not exceptional.

Contrary to Blanche's private thoughts, Eugenia felt very elegant. She wore a dress that had been cut down and skillfully made to fit. She could not know it was last year's style, and such a frivolous notion would have received a scoff from the practical Miss Dudley. The idea of discarding a perfectly attractive dress for some ruffle or yoke was beyond her comprehension, so she set out feeling delighted with her appearance. The gown was muslin with an apple-green spencer, and Eugenia's eyes glimmered like jade in its reflection and her pleasure. One would hardly notice her mouth was too full to be fashionable.

So Miss Dudley stepped out with a joyous demeanor quite uncommon in the poised and languid ladies of the ton. One was never to appear too interested, excited, delighted, or whatever bespoke effusiveness. Unaware of this subtlety, she presented a fresh and lively outlook.

Mrs. Rankin welcomed them as if they had returned from the gates of hell. "Oh, how good to see you! And this must be dear Miss Dudley. How grand to meet you, and may we offer our sympathy for your terrible ordeal? Come, meet my daughter, Lucy."

Lucy moved forward with a shy smile. A slender girl of pale description and coloring, she offered a softly spoken greeting, then glanced toward her mother to see if she had done it correctly. Fortunately, Mrs. Rankin offered a nod, and Lucy stepped back with a sigh of relief.

Noting and wondering about that odd exchange between mother and daughter, Eugenia made a pretty curtsy and took the proffered chair. She studied Miss Rankin's dress and coiffure, hoping to glean ideas for her future use. Before they had time to settle in with nondescript discussion, Mrs. Rankin launched directly to the subject of Eugenia's "rescue."

"You must tell me all! I should have died of fright to be lost in a snowstorm with a man I did not know," gushed Mrs. Rankin.

"Not at all, Mrs. Rankin, for Lord Grahame is a military man and capable of handling situations with authority. I was fortunate to have him escort me, for I was safe every minute," Eugenia replied with a clear note of gratitude.

Blanche struggled to maintain the placid expression on her face. She offered a benign smile as if all this were a perfectly normal occurrence. "Yes," she added, "we are delighted all turned out so well, and that Lord Grahame's ward has consented to a long visit with us. You can imagine how eager I am to show her London when the Season begins."

"You are going to take her to London?" Mrs. Rankin asked much too swiftly and with obvious surprise. She had allowed her shock to slip out. The incredulousness in her voice was there, plain and simple.

Blanche clenched her teeth and forced a smile. "But, of course, and *Thomas* is eager to join us. He needs a little diversion as well. You can imagine how occupied the poor dear has been since assuming the duties of his earldom. He has not had a moment to call his own. Luckily, I have convinced him he must come up to London and enjoy some entertainment the Season is sure to offer."

Mrs. Rankin, unaware that her lack of discretion had been noted, speculatively glanced toward her daughter, then to Blanche. "Lord Grahame is joining you in London? How divine. You *must* call upon us when you arrive, and of course attend Lucy's come-out ball. Miss Dudley will want some friends to enjoy what events . . . she wishes to attend. . . ."

The witch, thought Blanche. She is willing to tolerate Eugenia to have an opportunity to pursue Thomas for her insipid daughter. "Gracious yes! Thomas is eager to squire us. He is keen to be in *our* company, which surprises and delights me. Thomas is ever the grand companion."

Miss Rankin sat a little straighter, an interested gleam lighting her eyes. "Oh, how famous! We shall be quite cozy."

Mrs. Rankin sent a quelling look to her daughter. They would have to be on guard concerning the reception of Miss Dudley. They would not want to be seen first with her, if the tale of her remaining alone with the earl was to become common knowledge. The prudent action would be to wait and see how society accepted Miss Dudley before they took up with her. Still, Lord Grahame was undoubtedly a prime catch. They would not burn any bridges by mentioning the incident.

Blanche pursed her lips, for she had accurately read the calculating mind of Mrs. Rankin. "We must be about our other commitments. I did so want you to meet our new family member," Blanche said as she rose and nodded to Eugenia, who had been sitting more fascinated by the things not said than those that were.

The brisk air stung their cheeks as they emerged from the Rankin home, but it was anger that brought the pink to Blanche's cheeks. She no longer hid her feelings and allowed an affronted expression to settle on her face.

Eugenia hurried her steps to keep up with the long strides of her companion. It occurred to her that she inevitably found herself hurrying her steps to keep up with Lord Grahame and now found herself doing so with Blanche. Must be a family trait, she mused.

Eugenia waited to question Blanche until they had settled in the carriage. "Blanche, there were undercurrents I did not understand. It could not have been more evident that something was amiss, and that sort of thing terrorizes me. I am afraid of drawing-room discussions, since I lack any experience and could well be in the middle of some discussion with undertones I do not understand. This worries me when we go to London."

"All young girls worry when first they enter society. You have a presence about you that will keep you in good stead. As far as the drawing-room chatter, you will do just fine. You have the intelligence to act pointless, which is all a young lady needs.

"Pay no mind to *their* inferences, my dear. They are insignificant in the scheme of things. The Rankins exist on the fringes of London society, and they shall need us more than we need them. There is safety in that." Blanche forced a smile.

Somehow Eugenia did not think Blanche was being totally honest. "Is it because I am an orphan?" she asked.

"Heavens no," she lied. "You are the daughter of a national hero. The Dudleys have been an outstanding family since before Elizabeth's time. We will make the acquaintance of relatives you must surely have. Just because they have never shown any interest in you does not mean we cannot trade on their future acknowledgment once we establish ourselves in London."

"How do we know they will acknowledge me?"

"I shall see to it. Put them in a position that they would appear paltry if they did not."

"Blanche, I shall never go abegging. I learned early on to depend on none but myself. Believe me, it is the only way." Her voice was not hard, merely incisive.

Blanche did not answer; she could not. Things were worse than she had supposed. Thomas had gotten them in a pretty fix. He would have to rectify it. Eugenia deserved more.

It was only a matter of minutes after their return that Blanche was again ensconced with her brother. "Thomas, you cannot imagine Mrs. Rankin's not-so-subtle innuendo. I am appalled. You would have been furious if you had heard their snide comments. You simply must do something!

"Is the child so abhorrent to you that you could not consider her for a wife? You do not need wealth in your choice of wife. You have never been one to chase the ladies; at any rate, not so that I was aware."

Grahame laughed. "Blanche, you're a regular termagant. What am I to do? Do you really expect me to marry her? Why? She has already turned down my obligatory offer. That is sufficient. I promise, I will find her a suitable husband."

To his utter amazement, Blanche burst into tears. "Oh, she *is* a dear. You would have been so proud of her during the visit. I am very impressed by her. She is courageous, positive, honest, and intelligent. Thomas, you could do worse. You would be driven positively mad by the run-of-the-mill green girl. At least you can talk to this one!"

"You make her out as a paragon of virtue. She has certainly won you over. Which makes me point out that she will do as well in London. She will not need me, but I shall consider your words."

The Earl of Grahame sat at the head of the table, looking around at the dinner guests Blanche had invited to meet Eugenia. The vicar and his wife had shown Eugenia great kindness. Squire Heyward smiled benignly, but his wife had turned a cold shoulder to Eugenia. The Rankins and their insipid daughter had spent more time talking to him than to Eugenia. Blanche was correct, Eugenia fared well when compared to the simpering Lucy.

He had not yet appraised the other guests, for they had been exceedingly polite. He could not judge whether beneath those good manners lay a suspicious disapproval. The idea of mere country gentry making a belittling judgment irritated him. The protective feelings toward his ward increased this evening. By God, he thought, I will allow no cuts to her. His reasoning was brought to a halt by Mrs. Jennings's remarks.

"Miss Dudley," Mrs. Jennings said, "I am overwhelmed by your courage during your terrible ordeal. I quite admire you. I could never have survived so harrowing an experience. Imagine being lost in the snow and stranded in an empty cottage. Horrifying!"

The guests held their breath in one concerted effort. Silence fell and remained in command for a long awkward moment.

"Mrs. Jennings, you underestimate your ability. You must remember, Lord Grahame was there, and one could not worry with such a capable man." Eugenia's clear voice carried across the table.

"Under his aegis one could not but feel safe. I am fortunate, indeed. No, I was never fearful. Lord Grahame took control of a very difficult situation, and we survived. He was especially reassuring concerning the rats' nests in the cottage."

"Rats! There were rats?"

"Well, perhaps they were mice. . . . I cannot be sure."

Grahame noted a lifted eyebrow and a smirk on several faces. His pulse raced in a sudden spurt of anger. Those bastards, he thought, with their small, ugly minds, I shall give them something to talk about!

"The situation in which we found ourselves was frightening, to be sure. I wonder how many ladies could have managed such a harrowing experience?" Lord Grahame asked, and allowed his gaze to slip across every face.

A flutter of shaking heads and murmurs implied that never could *they* (meaning a true lady) survive so frightening an experience.

The earl's eyes narrowed when he noted the pride taken in the possibility of being so ladylike, one would perish rather than experience a misadventure. He was shocked. He looked to Eugenia and smiled. Her wonderful eyes, wide and understanding, met his. An affinity passed between them.

"So, you can see the fortunate opportunity I had to judge the mettle of my ward. I am exceedingly impressed and my admiration of her knows no bounds. The opportunities to know the true worth of a young lady are not found in rounds of dinners and balls. You can imagine my pleasure in learning my ward is a valiant heroine."

"But rats!" someone whispered.

"Well, perhaps not exactly rats," Eugenia said.

"Very *large* mice, I think," the earl said, and rose. He took his glass of wine and raised it. "I want you to join me in a toast. I had come to believe finding a worthy lady who did not faint dead away at the first sign of trouble was not possible. To my delight and everlasting gratitude, such an opportunity came to me when I went to fetch my ward. I could give my heart only to a lady of courage. So wish me well, Miss Dudley has agreed to marry me. I am most fortunate and thank providence for snow."

He reached over, took her hand, and raised her to her feet. He squeezed her trembling fingers and willed her to smile. He could feel her take hold and stiffen her back.

"My lord, you promised not to tell anyone so soon," she said with fluttering lashes and a modest tilt of her head.

Lord Grahame grinned. She even lies well, he thought, and sent her a speaking look, wondering if he would know if she ever lied to him. He doubted it, for she was the consummate actress. The idea amused him.

They stood smiling at each other with silly grins,

and an understanding passed between them. This, of course, was noted by the assembled guests. Observing the unspoken fondness that obviously existed between them, one could only judge that Lord Grahame was truly taken with the chit.

"So wish Eugenia well, and congratulate me for finding such a rare jewel." Lord Grahame said, and raised his glass to that of his guests.

Eugenia leaned over and Lord Grahame bent down to listen to her whisper. "Doing it a bit brown, my lord?"

"But of course," he said, and kissed her forehead.

The guests all began talking simultaneously, expressing good wishes and commenting on just how lucky the happy couple seemed.

Eugenia's eyes found Blanche's, and she noted the satisfied smile on the face of Grahame's sister. Eugenia smiled back, but she did not really understand what was going on around her. This sudden public proposal made her tremble. No way in the world could she refuse him now! Was that why he had done it? She looked at him, wondering what prompted his irrefutable offer. His glance slid over her, and she could glean nothing from his expression.

When the last guest had gone, Eugenia followed the earl to the bottom of the staircase. "My lord, why did you do that?"

"Because they took pride in their weakness and disdain in your bravery."

"But, my lord, you must not sacrifice yourself."

Their eyes met and held for a moment. He placed his hand on her shoulder. "Not now, Eugenia. Not tonight. I am weary and the pain in my leg is excruciating. Tomorrow we will talk."

She watched him slowly climb the steps, favoring his aching leg. The command in his demeanor was gone. She stood and watched until he disappeared at the top into the corridor that led to his bedchamber.

An overwhelming feeling of panic and loss filled her. She remembered standing alone in the great hall of the priory and she reached for her midriff. Her stomach turned in fear of her future. Was she doomed always to be the outsider? Was she forever to be in the situation of having to accept care given in duty? Never love? The pain was too much to bear. Lifting her skirts, she ran up the stairs to her room with tears of pity for him and herself.

Ten

The earl found his ward in the library. It was the first place he looked, and, as expected, she sat with her head buried in some formidable tome. Pale winter light surrounded her in an ethereal ambience, and she looked vulnerable when she raised her eyes to his entrance. He crossed the room and she smiled in greeting to him. He searched her face for a hint of her feelings, but none could be found.

"Good afternoon, Lord Grahame. I have been eager to see you all day. Why did you make the announcement? Was it because our adventure in the snowbound cabin is a topic of interest and therefore dooms you to an unwanted marriage? I cannot agree to it. You must send me to one of your estates. I can make myself useful by teaching the tenants' children and will be happy doing so. It is what I know best, not London."

"That is precisely why I spoke. The answer is not in sending you away. You are not some unworthy child to be cast aside at the first sign of trouble." He sat on the edge of the desk at which she sat.

"You declined my offer when last I asked, but I am convinced marriage is the only answer. I am asking you to reconsider. Many marriages are made for convenience to the family, for needs of title, funds, and land. Many survive in great comfort to both parties. The idea of romantic love is one of fleeting passion, and many fail in happiness because the emotion cannot remain for long." He watched her for a reaction and, seeing no rejection, continued.

"The best marriages, I suspect, are ones built on mutual respect and need. Blanche tells me I should marry to fill my nursery, and you are left to wagging tongues because I chose the worse possible day in which to fetch you."

"You can hardly be faulted for bad weather!" she exclaimed with affront to the injustice of such a charge.

He shrugged and continued. "I don't want a silly green goose of a girl for a wife. In fact, I should hate to have one. We were companionable in the time we spent alone. I should think we know more about each other than most who marry. I would not find it objectionable to have you for my wife. I want you to reconsider. You must remember that I have already told the world you will."

Eugenia stared at him. She had spent the night in torment, not knowing what he truly wished. She was sure he had been goaded into making the announcement out of some misguided sense of chivalry. Her mind raced with her pounding heart. She could find no better match, that was obvious. She knew she would like to marry him above all else, but therein lay the trap. Her heart could so easily give her away, and he was demanding a businesslike arrangement.

He waited for an answer. "Am I unacceptable to you?" he asked after her silence had lingered too long to be comfortable.

"Great heavens, no! You are most agreeable . . . I mean . . . you are far above my touch."

"You can dispense with that notion. Your father saved my father's life in Calcutta before he had the chance to sire me. You might say I owe my existence to your father, therefore it would be only fitting that I should . . . er . . . care for his daughter."

"I could never be happy being a duty."

"I know, and you shall never be that. I promise. I will want an heir and a spare, as is expected, but I shall not demand any more than you care to give. I speak bluntly, but it needs saying."

"Of course, my lord. I quite agree, and I should love children—above all else. I would not demand your affection, I want you to know."

"Agreed. I shall not demand yours either; still, it is to be understood I will not wear the horns for any man. You will remain true to this husband despite what is considered fashionable in some circles."

Eugenia blushed. She lowered her eyes and nodded. The idea of a lover was horrid, but she knew she was young and sometimes ladies became bored and . . . The school she attended was proof of that.

"If I say yes, I would pledge my fidelity."

"What do you mean, if you say yes? You do not like me?"

"Oh, yes, my lord. You are bonny, and I am exceedingly fond of you! I just do not like the idea. You must not sacrifice yourself for my honor."

"I decide that. Good, then it is agreed. We shall marry, and I will allow Blanche to take you to London for a little town polish and some fun. It will give you time . . . to . . . get used to the idea of marriage. I will come up to visit so as not to leave you to the speculation of an indifferent husband. They may say we married because of circumstances, but we will appear to be the happy couple. I truly think we can, given the framework. Do you agree?"

"Yes, my lord. You are too kind," she muttered, not knowing what else to say. Her life was changing too fast. From an orphan to a countess in a sentence, the idea was staggering.

He grabbed her arm and brought her to her feet. She raised her face in shock. "Never say that again," he demanded.

"Say what, my lord?" she asked with a pounding heart. His face with its glittering eyes was too close and his vehemence came unexpected.

"That I am marrying out of kindness, or duty," he demanded.

She could feel his breath on her cheek and trembled.

"Are you afraid of me?"

"Of course not, it is just all too much. It is all happening too fast. I can barely think."

He dropped his hand from her arm. He was sorry he had reacted so quickly. He just wanted her to agree and get on with it. He did not want hysterics.

His hand went to her cheek. "I am sorry. I want you to accept the marriage as the best for us. There is much we have in common. I am beginning to agree with Blanche, who thinks you are the best possible match for me."

Her eyes widened. "Really?"

"Really," he said, and bent his head. He placed a kiss somewhere between her lips and cheek, for Eugenia had turned her head when he leaned toward her. His hand cupped her chin, the other circled her waist, and he kissed her. She found herself kissing him back.

He stepped back and smiled. Crinkles appeared at the corners of his eyes, which flashed with amusement. "Now, that was not too distasteful, I trust."

"Not in the least, my lord," she said, and lowered her head lest he see her smile.

"I have instructed Blanche, or, rather, Blanche has instructed me, to turn you into a lady of fashionable proportions. Like the Jenny you once saw." His eyes rested on her in the most speculative way: Her heart fell to her shoes.

"I think I will call you Jenny. It could well be short for Eugenia, and we shall see that life offers you some joy."

She merely nodded, her eyes wide and the hint of tears at the corners. He reached over and patted her shoulder.

"Do not worry. All will be to your liking, I promise," he said as he walked to the door.

"What of you, Lord Grahame? Your happiness ought to count."

He turned just as he left the room and added, "It does."

The banns were immediately posted to allow for the wedding to take place before Lent. The date was set for February the twenty-third. Blanche was glad Easter was so late this year, as it allowed the three weeks before Lent and time for the wedding trip. Blanche brought two dressmakers into the manor to work in assembling the bride clothes for Eugenia.

"We shall choose the bare essentials until we get

to London and have a proper wardrobe made," Blanche explained as she held various fabrics next to Eugenia's face.

"Bare essentials?" Eugenia asked, wide-eyed at the vast array of fabrics already chosen for gowns to be made.

"Is there an echo in the room?" Blanche teased.

"Blanche, why so many gowns? What would I do with them?" Eugenia asked.

Blanche rolled her eyes to seek deliverance from heaven. "You will be the Countess of Grahame, and so must you appear to reflect on Thomas's great generosity."

"You are funning me. You mean people equate what I wear in direct proportion to Lord Grahame's regard?"

"Where did you learn such cant? Precisely. Now, stand still. What do you think of this for your traveling gown?"

"Blanche, I am weary. You choose. My head is a whirl."

"Go rest, Eugenia. I will finish."

Eugenia was only too glad to obey. The days were a haze of jumbled activity for the coming wedding, and she could no longer think. She needed to get away from all the activity. She knew it was cowardly not to remain in the middle of these decisions, but she did not even know what was appropriate, nor did she care. She would leave that to those who did.

Heading to the gallery, which held the portrait collection of ancestors to Lord Grahame, she knew she would be alone. It was a favorite escape for her. No one ever came here, so it was peaceful and she adored looking at the portraits to imagine what the subjects were like in life. One portrait drew her time and time again.

She moved to stand before the large portrait of a richly dressed cavalier who gazed down at her with a knowing eye. His eyes were pale and intense, and he seemed to fix them on her as if sending a message. He wore a mustache and Vandyke beard. His long dark hair curled on his lace-edged collar. The wide-brimmed hat sat rakishly on his head and sported an ostrich plume. The rich fabrics were painted in jewellike tones. His hand rested on his sword as if challenging the observer to note his competence in arms.

For some strange reason she felt drawn to this man. She stood lost in a trance as if she might answer the question in his eye.

"So you have found the founder of our family. My namesake, Thomas Winslow, defender of Charles the First. He was a valiant soldier, but allow me to show you another," Lord Grahame said.

Eugenia started at his words, which rudely interrupted her thoughts. "What? Oh, Lord Grahame. I did not hear you come up on me. You nearly frightened me to death."

"Thomas, my name is Thomas. My pardon for startling you. Would you like me to leave?"

"Heavens no, tell me about him."

Thomas's eyes traveled to the picture. "He fought for Charles the First against Cromwell. He escaped to France and joined in the Restoration. Charles the Second gave him these lands for his loyal service. A daring man whose greatest exploit was winning the hand of his wife. She was a lady of courage, not unlike you," he said, raising his hand to draw her attention to the lady in the painting next to the first Thomas Winslow.

Eugenia gazed at the lady who stood with feet firmly planted. Her gaze was not of things worldly. She was dressed in a full-skirted gown of black with a large collar trimmed in Brussels lace. She wore a white cap and her honey-colored hair cascaded in ringlets around her face. She had clear blue eyes and a sweet mouth in a serene face.

"Her name was Sarah and she was the daughter of Lord Bradley, who was MPS of Herefordshire and away in London on parliamentary affairs. She refused to surrender the castle to my father's troops. A total of seven hundred troops faced the beleaguered garrison. They began a siege and in the evening, as was custom. Next, they sent a message for her to surrender the castle in the name of the high sheriff of the city of Hereford. My father worded the summons in the kindest of terms.

"She sent her reply: 'Tell your commander, who preys on hapless women, to take his army and leave forthwith. I will not surrender what is my home. The King has promised liberty, and I defend in the law of reason and liberty.'

"Lord Winslow drew up his horse and demanded she quit the castle, promising to place guards to protect the property. She came to the door and said, 'It is in all likelihood you will protect me out of all I own.'

"My ancestor must have shifted sheepishly in his saddle, but he still threatened her. 'If you remain willful, you may suffer and know you have brought it on yourself.'

"We are told, she tossed of her head and defiantly replied, 'Good sir, I cannot agree. I have not discharged these bullies to prey on helpless women in their very homes.'

"Thomas fell in love at that moment. He withdrew his troops but vowed to return to claim the beauty who had defied his army.

"During the exile he returned from France in disguise. He wooed the lady and married her. I will save that story for another day."

"I have never heard such a story. How marvelous!" Eugenia looked back at Sarah with new interest. Yes, she thought, the lady would defy an army. She smiled and turned to Grahame.

"I am much enchanted, my lord."

"Now, you can agree, that it is my Winslow duty to also marry a lady of valiant heart."

"Lord Grahame, I will not have you equate my self-serving act to stay alive with that of this brave lady. I shall, however, keep her in mind when traversing the frightening ballrooms of London."

Grahame laughed.

Eleven

Eugenia Dudley stood before the cheval mirror on her wedding day. She resolutely gazed at her pale reflection with fear of the unknown and nervously touched her small cameo broach. From the reflection one could almost believe she had been pampered all her life. The creamy silk of her gown hung in slender folds from the high empire waist. The square neck of her bodice was edged with a web-fine lace frill. The wedding dress, provided by Blanche, was exquisite, and it shimmered as if transported from some heavenly realm.

And that is exactly how Eugenia felt—a transplant *to* some foreign and heavenly realm. It was difficult getting used to the changes that were coming too rapidly to contemplate, let alone assimilate. Grahame might call her Jenny, as he did in recent days, but inside remained the little lost Eugenia who had entered a school for displaced children so many years before.

She tried to shake off the dreadful feeling. She looked very well indeed, but she would soon step through that door on her way to the chapel and become the Countess of Grahame. She placed her hand on her midriff; the silk under her fingers was soft and pleasing, but only aggravated the feeling that she was about to throw up.

How could she be so ungrateful? They had done everything they could to make her welcome. Lord Grahame was sacrificing his happiness to protect her name. She scoffed aloud, for whatever did her reputation mean in the event of another's unhappiness? She could not go through with it. How could she? Even worse, how could she cry off? Guests were now assembling; she could not insult Lord Grahame for all the world to see. Oh, how could she have been lulled into this selfish adventure? Had she been lulled? Or had her own selfish desires . . . ? Tears welled. She put her hand to her mouth just as the door flew open. The distraction mollified the nausea. Blanche entered, preceded by her three lively daughters who had arrived with their father for the wedding.

Eugenia smiled. One could hardly help doing so, for the children were adorable.

"Ah, that is gratifying . . . to see you smiling, that is. I half expected to see you moping about. Well, thank God for that," Blanche said, warily examining the pinched white face of the bride. She sighed and thought, the saints be praised it will soon be over. There were times she despaired of the wedding ever taking place. That is why she had remained at Windhaven when she had wanted to return to Tower Hall.

People are odd, she thought, cannot see what is plain before their eyes. Well, both Thomas and Eugenia would have to find the truth themselves. Informing one of whom one loves seldom edifies.

The girls danced about in excitement, totally removing from Eugenia the morose mood that had recently gripped her. She laughed. We are funny creatures, to be lifted by the entrance of laughing children from the depths of despair to acceptance, she mused. She was horrified by this truth and doubted her sincerity. The idea that her regrets were not sincere bothered her.

"Blanche, am I doing the right by your brother?"

"Does the word *ninny* strike you? It should, for you sound like one. Thomas would have procrastinated on getting a wife until he was old and crotchety. He has been in the military too long. What does he know about life? Barracks? Guns? Drills? Actually, you have saved him from some horrible fate, I assure you. He would have waited until the last minute, then chosen whoever was standing next to him at some assembly that he had got himself to in order to find a wife. Or worse than that, some scheming mother would inveigle him into a life with a woman with a pretty face and a whining mouth. She would complain that having children ruined her figure, she would present him with a pale, thin child and then hightail it to London for the Season."

Eugenia was enchanted by this exaggerated speech and giggled in utter delight. "Great heavens, how you carry on!"

"You laugh! In disbelief, too! *But I know Thomas*, and I have not missed the mark. So that is settled. Let us look at you." She took Eugenia's hands and held them. "You look divine. He will thank his lucky day for snow."

Tears again threatened. Eugenia was smiling and crying, raw emotions crowding in at once.

"None of that, child. We will have no puffy eyes. Keep the smile and dispense with the tears. For to tell the truth, I have made this match to please myself. I wanted a choice in a sister." She kissed Eugenia on the cheek.

"Girls, quiet, quiet now. Cease your running about or you will muss your new dresses," Blanche ordered as she turned and grabbed for the first girl she could reach.

Both stopped and stood still, beaming with excitement. "Aunt Jenny, you look like a princess," Rose said with Violet and Myrtle agreeing.

Blanche beamed approval. "Maybe it is working," she said.

"What is working, Blanche?" Eugenia asked.

"I named the girls in hopes it would reflect on their behavior."

"Behavior?"

"Yes, Rose . . . sweet, Violet . . . shy, and Myrtle . . . noble. Do not think it is clever?"

"Oh, Blanche, you could send the blue devils away from the devil himself. By all means it is working; they are adorable. You are fortunate."

"You would think others would discover the idea," Blanche teased in feigned seriousness.

"I shall keep it in mind for my children," Eugenia said. Then, wondering about her future children, that ominous feeling started to return.

Blanche forestalled that by commanding Eugenia to hold still while she pinned the circle of flowers in her hair.

Thomas Charles Carlisle Winslow, the Earl of Grahame, married Miss Dudley by the power invested in the very Reverend Marcus Willowby, in the lovely baroque chapel at Windhaven. Struggling desperately not to tremble, Miss Dudley stood dwarfed by the earl, who seemed as calm as could be reasoned. She took a shy peek to see if he was affected by this momentous occasion. She expected to see a frown but caught a casual expression, as if he did this sort of thing every day! How could he be so relaxed, she wondered, and leaned closer as the cleric addressed his lordship on his desire to unite in matrimony. Grahame gave Eugenia's hand a squeeze that made her start ever so slightly. She could see his lips turn up at the corners. He is enjoying this, she thought, aghast. She turned her eyes straight ahead and put her mind to the task of becoming a wife. Men, they were a complete enigma!

The assembly was small and filled with those who seemed to wish them well. Even some servants shed a tear as they watched from the back of the chapel. It was rewarding to them to see an unaffected young lady reach such heights.

Blanche sat beside her husband and children and smiled as satisfied as if it were her own sister making so suitable a match. She had missed being away from her family, but the reward of seeing Thomas safely married was worth every minute. She would accompany Eugenia to London, but Lloyd and the children would be with her. She sighed contentedly, and Lloyd reached over to give her hand a pat.

The celebration breakfast held in the beautiful dining room showed Blanche's careful attention to detail. Spring flowers that had been forced into bloom graced the tables and window ledges. An omen, as if to proclaim the promising future of the wedding couple.

The famous Grahame gold plate sat gleaming on the pristine linen table covers. Candles flickered, offering a warm glow against a cool gray light that filtered in through the leaded glass of the high mullioned windows. The scene had been played out in this room for generations of Grahames. That timeless tie to the past offered the comfortable promise that life would continue in the same unending procession of future earls.

Guests were lavished with delicate dishes that appeared in unending variety. The merriment of the guests mounted as profuse toasts were offered to the couple.

The earl sat with a calm demeanor and accepted all toasts, even those that grew in subtle ribaldry and great good humor. Eugenia sat frozen, that is to say, her smile remained frozen on her face. Her heart pounded. Her mouth was dry and her hands sweaty, and she frowned.

"My dear Jenny, it would suit my purposes if you could manage to look a bit more pleased," Grahame whispered as he bent over to her. The guests clapped and cheered, sure he was offering some romantic idea to his suitably shy wife.

She raised her enormous hazel eyes to his lordship's. They carried a plea, fear, and entreaty of protection all in one devastating look. Lord Grahame almost dropped the glass of wine he had just raised in toast to her. His jaw muscle tightened, and his eyes flickered with emotion that was unreadable.

The Earl of Grahame, who was known for his fearless valor in battle, trembled with fear of the future. Great God, what am I about? All his original dread rushed in. It was a mistake. He should have found her a husband who did not frighten her to death.

Reaching over, he took her hand to his lips, to the great enjoyment of his guests. "You have nothing to fear from me, Eugenia," he said, placing a kiss in the palm of her cold hand.

"My lord, I know that."

He waited for her to say something more. He watched her, and she remained silent. A peak of resentment surfaced. He had done all that could be expected. He had shown her kindness and offered her words to allay her fears. What in the hell more did she want? He withdrew his hand and sat back in his chair. He remained quiet for several minutes, absently rubbing his nagging leg, then rose with his raised glass.

He turned to smile at her, but it was a smile of no meaning. His eyes glinted cold; the warrior stood before them with his glass raised.

"A parting toast. I thank you all for joining in our happy wedding day. My friends, we thank you. And now, if you will excuse us, we are about to make our good-byes."

He reached down and brought Eugenia to her feet. "Say your good-byes, my lady," he whispered.

"Yes, thank you for all your good wishes. We are pleased to have you share . . . wedding celebration. . . ."

A flurry of kisses, wishes, and good-byes were made before the Earl and Countess of Grahame were able to depart.

Twelve

Ensconced in a green velvet cloak lined with sable, Eugenia rested against the comfortable squabs of the earl's traveling coach. Her feet, in green leather half-boots, rested on a warming stool, and her hands, in matching leather gloves, were tucked in a magnificent sable muff. Diamond and emerald earrings, a gift from her husband, sparkled on her ears with each movement of her head. However, the elegance of her dress occupied no place in her thoughts.

The day was misty cold, the air hung with droplets of moisture, and ice crystals lay on the thawing earth, which offered the first hint of spring waiting in the wings. The world appeared as a canvas painted in tones of gray, casting a dispiriting atmosphere.

Despite the cold bleakness of this day, no chill reached the new Countess of Grahame, so richly and warmly dressed. Yet an icy knot gripped her heart that had nothing to do with the gray weather. She was exasperated whenever she caught a glimpse of her husband as he rode beside the coach. He had elected to ride on his stallion, and she suspected it was being with her in the confines of the coach that had prompted his choice.

Eugenia could not be sure it was contention that set him to brave the weather, but she surmised as much. He was annoyed; the reason could be his enforced sacrifice to society's conventions. This was her fault. She should have refused and not given in to the seduction of the solution that offered her a comfortable life at his expense. Her acceptance was proving to be no solution, and she regretted her lack of seeing beyond their entreaties of the future. Closing her eyes against her growing guilt, she rested against the seat.

They were en route to his lordship's hunting box to spend the first days of their marriage. Time alone, to get to know each other, was to be their wedding trip. A small, snug hunting box would be ideal for lovers, but for strangers such proximity boded disaster. What would he expect of her? She raised her chin at the thought. This unobserved gesture of defiance was indulged since there was none to take issue.

She could easily imagine the joy a wedding trip would be for a couple lucky enough to marry for love. Arranged marriages forced an intimacy between strangers that could only be strained at best. A perfect example could be seen in the marriage of the Prince and Princess of Wales. They were known to be miserable with each other.

The idea of one parti being reluctant brought a shudder to her. How did women over the millennium suffer such treatment? They had. She knew full well such an arrangement had as much chance of happiness as a toss of dice; some fared well, others were pure hell on earth. While she could well imagine hers would be no hell at the hands of some abusive bully, it was no less terrifying to know one's husband had been forced into the marriage.

What would it be for a man to take a woman he did not fancy? She shuddered. Her mind raced on. A woman forced to choose someone abhorrent ... but ... Lord Grahame was no ogre. No aversion racked her, and deep within her being lay the undeniable emotion that could be her undoing. She harbored no reluctance, only the unspoken truth that the marriage pleased her. Lord Grahame pleased her very well indeed. A quiver ran through her, and she blushed with chagrin at the danger of her feelings. She vowed to be a good wife, but she would have to be heedful of her heart.

Glimpsing Lord Grahame astride his magnificent stallion, a resolute tightness set on his face, she lowered her eyes. She had spent years hiding her thoughts, had grown up doing so, and she could do it again. With luck she could do it again.

They had been traveling roads through the watery fields dotted with the slender streams of Hampshire. The foggy gray world seemed to offer a mystery of hidden history and centuries of cultivation. The terrain offered easy access with its gently sloping landscape and had done so throughout the ages. It held a history of armies that had come to conquer and peoples who came to stay.

The route became barely passable when they turned off the main road unto a narrower track. Although the coach was well sprung, Eugenia bounced as the wheels took the rutted road and her creeping nausea grew. The trek narrowed and headed up a knoll into a stand of beech woods. A charming ivy-covered brick house stood in a meadow surrounded by woods. A winter garden lay bare, but the image of riotous flowers, come spring, was evident. In fact, tiny green shoots of flowering bulbs were visible scattered among the dead leaves of autumn. The coach halted at the entrance.

Lord Grahame swung down from his horse and moved to the coach door as Ben jumped down. "We have arrived, as you can see," he said, letting down the steps and extending his hand. She placed her hand in his and awkwardly emerged from the coach. She stood looking up at the house obviously built during the reign of William of Orange, for it boasted a stepped roofline.

"My lord, the house is enchanting," she said with awe emanating from her eyes. She glanced to him and smiled. "I tell you now, I shall remain forever."

He made no comment but took her arm and proceeded to escort her up the brick path. The front door flew open and two servants emerged with broad grins of welcome.

"Welcome, Lord Grahame," the rotund servant said as he studied his new mistress with unabashed interest.

"My dear, this is Mr. and Mrs. Beekans. They will quite spoil us during our stay."

Mrs. Beekans dropped a curtsy. "We are honored to meet you, my lady."

Eugenia liked the twinkle in her eye and the ruddy country glow about her face. These were no haughty servants known to abound in the fine houses. It was a relief, for she did not begin to know how to deal with servants. She had much to learn.

"Come in, come in, or you are likely to catch your death. This cold goes right through you," Mrs. Beekans said, and scurried ahead into the house. Mr. Beekans brought up the rear.

"I've baked your favorite lemon sponge cake and raspberry tarts," Mrs. Beekans pridefully informed the earl when they crossed the threshold.

"I often dream of your cakes and could think about nothing else all the way here," Lord Grahame said.

Lucky for *him*, Eugenia thought wryly, wishing her thoughts had been equally imperturbable.

He turned to Eugenia. "If you think the house is wonderful, wait until you have tasted Mrs. Beekans's cooking. Now, there is a reason to stay forever!"

"You are a flatterer, to be sure," Mrs. Beekans replied, but she was enormously pleased.

Eugenia was touched by the housekeeper's obvious devotion to the earl, knowing such esteem can only be earned. She glanced to the earl. He was smiling, and the transformation was touching. The warmth, humor, and teasing eyes were something she had never seen before. She had seen him smile in amusement, but this warmth was unprecedented. He looked ten years younger! He turned to her and the expression faded. The obvious implication stung like a slap.

"Mrs. Beekans will show you to the bedchamber. Perhaps you would like to rest a bit before I show you about," he said with a slight nod before departing.

The feeling of abandonment at being left standing in an unfamiliar hall again flooded her. She blushed at the helpless feeling and turned to the speculative gaze of Mrs. Beekans. "I should like that very much. The excitement of the wedding and the journey were tiring," she managed to utter, then trailed behind the broad back of the housekeeper to her first bedchamber as a married woman.

Eugenia was not sure what a chalet might look like, but she imagined it could not be far from this charming house. She marveled when she entered the framed and whitewashed room with its chintz fabrics and crackling, merry fire. No spectacular elegance and pride of procession were evident here, only cozy, welcoming comfort. Her eyes traveled the room, noting the sloping ceiling and windows of diamond-shaped leaded glass with window seats flanking each end of the room. It was a house of considerable romantic imagination. Whose? Not her warrior husband's, she was sure, but then, she had just seen a glimpse of his kindliness toward his servants. Perhaps she should wait to make such judgments.

She crossed the room with tentative steps and stood next to the large four-poster, her hand closed on the carved post in unconscious need for support. She had allowed herself to be led willingly with only unconvincing demur because her secret was in her desire to accept his offer. Where before she had been directed, she now had to assume the initiative of a willing wife and did not know where to begin.

She had been married only hours and already had managed to irritate her husband. It was obvious he had perceived some slight, and she had no idea of its source.

She removed her cloak and bonnet and placed them on the bed. Turning and catching her reflection in a cheval mirror, she was shocked at the pale, peaked face that stared back. Crossing to stand before the mirror, she smoothed her hair and pinched her cheeks to bring a bit of color. There was little in her reflection that pleased. She wished, for the first time in her life, that she were beautiful.

A soft knock at the door brought Mrs. Beekans carrying a tray with piping hot soup, crusty bread, and tea. "You must be frozen, so I have brought a wee bit to restore you. A trip on rough winter roads would undo a saint," Mrs. Beekans said as she set the tray on a small table. "Come sit and have a bite."

Eugenia obeyed with a wan smile. At least it gave her something to "do." She hated just standing around in this bedroom, not knowing what to do next. She was uncomfortable, not knowing her place and how she should act. It was all too foreign, and she was afraid of failing.

The aroma wafting up made her realize just how hungry she was. She welcomed the distraction and took a chair at the table. The soup was delicious, and the warmth coursed through her veins, causing her spirits to lift.

"Is his lordship about?" Eugenia asked, hating herself but unable to refrain from posing the question.

"Nay, he's gone off to the kennels and stables," Mrs. Beekans replied, then added, "He said he would join you for dinner after you have rested from your journey."

Eugenia wondered if she heard a hint of curiosity in the servant's voice. Mrs. Beekans curtsied and left her alone.

It was a relief to be alone and terrifying at the same time. She could not hide in some bedroom the rest of her life because it was safe! She would have to step forward and meet her new life. But she would wait and see what was expected and react to that. It was like being in a game and not knowing the rules; she would have to seek her way cautiously.

Thirteen

Lord Grahame shivered in the chilly dampness of the late afternoon air. He had just become aware of the nipping cold. Shadows creeping across the ground reminded him of the time. Shifting his weight to favor his aching leg, he drew his collar up around his ears.

I best start back, he thought. The time spent in inspecting the kennels and visiting the stables had temporarily put the reality of the day from his mind. That was only an illusion. His eyes flickered; little more than time spent in mere postponement of the fact he must face the prospects of his marriage. What was it to be? Could they make it at least comfortable?

He turned his steps toward the house. Why had he allowed the pressure of society and his sister to prevail? Eugenia had given him his chance by first refusing him. Pity, he felt pity for the waif of a girl. He felt guilty about that. Still, there was something else, something shadowy and obscure that had led him to accept this marriage. He was not one to go against his own wishes. He never had. He could not put his finger on it.

She was pleasant, and he liked the challenge of

her mind. Was that enough to build on? How did she view the situation?

His grim thoughts trod at his heels as he trudged along the path. Ice mingling with thawing mud squished under his boots. Favoring his tired, aching leg, he walked on with his hands in his pockets and his head bent. If he were aware of his dejection, his demeanor was proof.

He tried to imagine his future with Eugenia, but no image suggested itself. It did not seem real. He could not imagine the future. It lay in the unknown tomorrow, shadowed with no hint given.

During any pending battle that lay before him, he had weighed the known to form an appraisal of the outcome. He would determine the size of the forces against him, their position, and their ordnance. The best weapon lay in knowing the mind of his opponent. With these facts he made his plans of attack. Could he equate that experience to his marriage?

Thomas smiled at the equating of marriage to battle, but then, he was not the first to do so. Go slowly, he told himself. Learn more about Eugenia, weigh their situation, then decide just what possibilities existed. More than that, find out what he wanted out of it. Suspended in indecision, he headed back to the hunting lodge.

Eugenia stood in the parlor, waiting in apprehension. She had no idea when to expect Lord Grahame. Waiting for his return had been unnerving, and she faulted him for this.

She had dressed carefully in a warm gown of soft green wool. The sleeves were gathered at the shoulders and the high neck was trimmed with lace.

Blanche had kindly provided her wardrobe, and Eugenia was profoundly grateful. She could not have faced the earl otherwise. To be a beggar was humbling enough, but to be shabby was now unthinkable. The need to appear at her best had never been a consideration before, but now it was of paramount importance. She hated the implications of the shallowness such thoughts indicated. She had always held herself above that sort of thinking.

She drew the shawl around her shoulders and glanced around the attractive room for the hundredth time. The dancing flames sent a cheerful note and flickering shadows along the walls in the dying light of day. A table set charmingly before the fire had been the busy afternoon endeavor of Mrs. Beekans. It did look appealing and romantic, sitting with sparkling crystal and candles. An intimate dinner for two was the evening offering of Lord Grahame's two faithful servants.

Eugenia eyed the scene warily. The enforced message was undeniable, and it gave her stomach flutters. How should she act? Reserved? No, he would think her ungrateful. Friendly and cheery? He would see through that and think her witless, or perhaps admire her effort to look on the positive side. She paced the floor and worried herself into a panic. She would have to think of *something*, she told herself.

Eugenia turned at the sound of Lord Grahame's entrance. He was dressed in a dark coat that accentuated his dark good looks. His eyes flickered, but she could not read their meaning. He gave her a brief nod and crossed the room to stand near her.

"I hope you rested well. The wedding and journey were taxing for you," he said. His forced words were constrained, and she felt the speculation behind them. His gaze then scanned the room and came to rest on her as if waiting for some comment.

"Yes, Lord Grahame, I rested. This lodge is welcoming and comfortable. I could be contented here."

"Good. You avoid my given name. Call me Thomas."

"Yes, my lord," she answered, trying to be agreeable while controlling her racing heart. She was overwhelmed by the situation and at a loss as to what to do and say.

An eyebrow arched over his penetrating gray eyes. "Whose idea . . . yours?" he asked with an indicating wave of his hand.

Eugenia's eyes followed his direction to the festive table so cozily set by the fire. She blushed at the implication that the idea had been hers. "Mrs. Beekans thought it would be romantic for the newlyweds. I could hardly decline."

If Lord Grahame noted her trembling voice, he gave no indication. "Sherry?" he asked, taking up a crystal decanter. He proceeded to pour some golden liquid into the delicate glass.

"Yes!"

Lord Grahame smiled as he handed her the glass. "A little dutch courage, eh?"

Her hazel eyes flashed a defiant green spark, then faded into a veil of unreadable expression. He delighted in the change of her eyes from green to gold and deeper. It was worth challenging her just to see them vary.

He raised his glass in salute. "Here is to the hope that our venture will prove agreeable to us both."

Before Eugenia could answer, the door opened

and Mr. and Mrs. Beekans entered with a rolling cart. Covered dishes were placed on the trestle table to be used as a sideboard for their meal.

"Smells wonderful. I did not realize I am so hungry. Surprising how one's wedding sharpens one's appetite. Don't you agree, my dear?"

Eugenia stared at him with an expression implying he belonged in Bedlam. Her hand rested on her fluttering stomach, as if to calm it, and he chuckled.

The two servants bustled about, arranging the dishes. They placed the first course of rich oyster stew on the table. Upon completing their task, they bowed. "We shall excuse ourselves, your lordship. We will return early tomorrow to clear away," Mrs. Beekans said with a curtsy and a beaming smile. The servants lived in a cottage on the grounds and would leave the lodge to the earl and his new wife to enjoy in undisturbed privacy.

Lord Grahame gave them a nod. "Yes, that is all for tonight. We appreciate your efforts." He watched them leave, then turned to Eugenia. "Shall we?"

He helped her into a chair. They ate the stew in silence. Next came roast hen with a variety of side dishes, all carefully prepared.

Lord Grahame put away a complimentary amount of food, a tribute to Mrs. Beekans. Eugenia picked at it. It was delicious, but there just wasn't room. She could barely swallow. Grahame gave no notice of her slim appetite, and she was grateful for that.

Later they sat before the fire, each with a small brandy. The meal had been without conversation for the most part. Only the smallest, most trivial comments had passed between them. They now sat in the same strained silence.

When they were stranded, they talked with great freedom. Now the events brought an awareness that seemed insurmountable.

"Lord Grahame, are you annoyed at something I have done? Have I offended you?"

He was surprised at the suddenness of her question. The directness showed her courage. Their eyes met.

"No," he answered. She knew he lied.

"It would seem I have," she said.

"You must call me Thomas," he said.

"Thomas, you must tell me how to go about what you expect, and I shall endeavor to please you."

"My, my, that is quite a speech."

"Lord Grahame, you must not mock my efforts. I mean to make you a good wife."

"I've no doubt of that. You are an earnest little chit. I have no idea what I want in a wife; I have never had one. I suppose I should like us to be agreeable. I suspect it is the best we can hope for."

Eugenia dropped her gaze. He did not seem the same man she had been stranded with. The tension between them precluded any ease.

"Yes, I suppose you are correct."

A falling log caught their attention, and they sat staring at the fire for a while. The clock ticked away the minutes.

"Lord Grahame . . . er . . . Thomas, you did seem annoyed when we left the wedding breakfast. I just know you were. How can I correct any manner that might distress you if I don't know what it is?"

"I see I have a persistent wife. Now, how shall I

deal with that?" he asked, trying to offer a teasing response.

"Persistent?"

He sighed, as all men do when their wives insist on pursuing a subject best left alone. In fact, it was a failing found in most women, or at least that was his perception. "Yes, I have already answered your question."

"Not really, you set it aside."

"You are doing it again."

"Doing what?"

"Insisting I answer the question with the answer you no doubt have formulated in your mind!"

"But you *were* annoyed!"

"I was overwhelmed by our prospects. I am sure the same thoughts occurred to you."

She nodded agreement. "Do you think we can manage? I mean, to deal well together?" she asked with a frown wrinkling her brow and concern clouding her eyes.

"We are not children. We have made a concession to the dictates of society, which, by the way, I think ludicrous. But to answer your question, yes, we can deal well together. Providing you do exactly as I order," he said.

She glanced sharply at him. She could not tell if he was funning, or fobbing her off. "But of course, my lord. I cannot imagine anyone going at odds to you. Least of all me."

Now it was his turn to wonder if she was teasing. He could not tell. Those large eyes gazed at him in heavenly innocence. He felt a traveling sensation that took him by surprise. His eyes meandered along her face and across her slender, very feminine form. The idea surprised him.

"Well, it has been a long day, and I think we have the rest of our lives to find out how well we deal together. Let us retire. I am weary."

"But, your lordship, we have to settle so many things."

"Tomorrow, Eugenia, tomorrow."

Fourteen

Eugenia's nervous fingers fumbled with the tiny buttons on her lawn nightdress. Since no personal servants had been brought along, she had to muddle through on her own. The idea brought an ironic smile to her full mouth. Only days before, she had been uncomfortable with the ministrations of a lady's maid. She had felt so out of place with a hovering servant. All her life she had been quite capable of dressing herself, as any fool could. Now, when her fingers refused to obey, she wished for such assistance. The idea amused her and for a moment lightened her distress.

She slipped into a soft velvet robe of green and tied the belt. It was delightfully warm against her shivering body, and she hugged herself with the sybaritical pleasure of the soft fabric. Luxury is seductive, she thought. She would have to guard against the pitfalls of indulgence. Few prospered by vanity, she primly told herself, recalling the strictures of the upbringing that still haunted her mind. Oh, but it is such fun to own something so luscious, a tiny voice seemed to whisper.

Seating herself before the dressing table, she ran her fingers against her cheeks, shocked by the pale face that stared back. Had she appeared this way before Lord Grahame? She tried on a smile but managed only to look foolish and false. He must not see her like this! Perhaps he would not come to her; after all, that was their agreement. She relaxed momentarily with the notion he would honor their arrangement. Can you be sure? she asked herself.

Trying to dispel her futile thoughts, she unpinned her braid and furiously began to brush her hair. What next, she wondered, and a flood of color reached her cheeks. Her hands trembled as she brushed out her long hair. She caught the reflection of the bed in the background and wondered if, perhaps, he would come and whether he would expect her to . . .

The door opened and the personification of her thoughts entered the room. Her brush paused in midair. Grahame was wearing a loose-fitting dressing gown over what she assumed to be a nightshirt. The shirt was open at the throat and dark hair showed below the strong column of his neck. She knew he was a powerful man but never had he seemed so overwhelmingly so. His masculinity was as vivid as a blinding noonday sun. Her temples pulsated with her pounding heart. When he crossed the room and stood looking down at her, she dropped her gaze and returned to her brisk brushing.

"I did not realize your hair had such golden lights," he said, touching the silky strands. A shiver went down her spine. Grahame dropped his hand and backed away.

Eugenia replaced the brush, gathered up the strands of hair, and rapidly began to plait it. He withdrew from her and began to amble around the room, hesitant in his manner but saying nothing more. His unspoken words seemed to dominate the air as if they had been spoken. She wondered what he was thinking.

He picked up a crystal orb and examined it. He replaced it on the inlaid table, then turned and looked at her.

Eugenia finished, sighed, and rose from the bench. With an air of someone resigned to face fate, she moved to stand before him. Folding her hands in front her, she waited, not knowing what to say. She did not know what she was supposed to say in such an uninformed situation. Expectantly waiting for him to say something, do something, she rested her eyes on his chest. She could not bring herself to look into his eyes.

A flicker of amusement crossed his winter-gray eyes. She bravely stands her ground, he thought in admiration.

"Are you afraid of me?" he asked. His words fell like a whisper.

"No, not of you, only the situation . . . I had not thought . . . that is . . ."

"That I might seek my husbandly rights?" He smiled as his gaze searched her face.

Green flashed in her eyes. He was toying with her or, at least, she thought he was. The beast. "Precisely, my lord."

"Ah, the prim Miss Dudley appears before my eyes."

"Lord Grahame, we agreed this was to be a marriage of necessity. I am willing to do my duty when it comes to children, but we . . ."

He threw back his head and laughed. The laugh died as suddenly as it came. "I will not subject my unwanted presence upon my so *willing* bride." Rancor tinged his words.

She shivered and raised her hand as if to protest. He cut her words before they crossed her lips. "Come, get into bed. I shared a bed with you before and now find myself married to you. Do you not think it ironic, I am denied the very thing for which I was suspected of doing?"

"My lord, if you insist, I shall, of course . . ."

"But I do not insist." He turned to her, his eyes flashing. "Eugenia, *do not do me any favors.* I seek none." He pulled down the bed cover. "Now, get in."

She obeyed, scampering across the space between them and climbing into the huge bed. She stretched out, her body rigid and trembling. He pulled the covers over her, then stood a second longer, looking at her. Their eyes held a moment, and she wished she knew what he was thinking. Those gray eyes of ice and fire glittered; what was behind them?

She watched him slowly move around the bed to the opposite side. Provokingly slow, she thought. He is purposely antagonizing me. She watched him slowly remove his dressing gown, then draw back the covers. He gave her a charmingly disarming smile, then proceeded to climb in next to her. Her mind was racing so fast, no thought stayed long enough to register. He made several exaggerated adjustments getting comfortable, but remained carefully apart from her. Their bodies did not touch.

"I'll stay but a moment. We would not want the servants to think their master was kept from his wedding bed. I shall sleep in the dressing room when the bed looks as though I have spent the night with my bride." The sting of his rancor hung in the dim room.

They lay side by side in a silence that was worse than the rancor. Enmity was something she could hold on to, but silence was intangible and harder to assess. Should she say something? What? It was becoming more distressing by the moment to know she brought a loveless marriage to him. Should she reach out to him? No, for she obviously did not evoke any passion. What could she say?

She remained still. If only she had been stronger and not tempted by the security offered her. Their arguments had seemed so logical at the time, and she had believed them because she had wanted to believe. If she were really honest, she admitted, Lord Grahame was the actual inducement. Just to belong to him in whatever way. She squeezed her eyes tight to ward off tears and her thoughts.

When Eugenia heard his even breathing, her rigid body began to relax. Thank God, he is asleep. She sighed a prayer of thanksgiving. All that blatant masculinity was just too much to contemplate; she would have to eventually, but not now, not tonight.

Recent events had taken their toll, and an overwhelming weariness flooded her body and being. The warmth of the bed brought on a drowsiness, and she, too, drifted into a blessed sleep of oblivion.

Lord Grahame was not sleeping. He lay staring into the dark of the room, lit only by the glow of the fireplace. He was conscious of her tense body and knew the minute she began to relax and fall asleep. He had made some progress.

He was a virile man, and he found his wife to be more appealing with each day he knew her. Yet he had promised. Damn his promises; he should demand his rights! But he knew he could not take a woman in need only, especially one who showed reluctance.

He was not in love with her, but he sure wouldn't mind making love to her. His night stretched out before him in frustrated torment. He rose and slipped from the bed. The cool air reached his skin, and he softly muttered a curse. He would seek the solace of the dressing room, which held no soft, warm body to tempt him. He quietly left the room.

Sometime between the night and the gray dawn that meets morning, Eugenia stirred. Half awake, she became aware that Lord Grahame was no longer in bed. He had kept his promise and probably had gone to the dressing room to sleep. She slid her hand under the warm covers to where he had lain. The empty space was cold, and she pulled her hand back as if she had touched fire, and she realized he had been gone for some time.

A foolish tweak of disappointment touched her. Dispelling the thought with a disgust of herself, she rolled over and hugged her pillow. She was tired and overwhelmed by the strangeness of the circumstance. It was her duty to be a wife to Lord Grahame. She had failed in that duty.

What should she have done? Just how did one go about such an event? Besides, he told her that he wanted no favors from her. She could hardly foist herself on him, now could she? Her thoughts sounded hollow and she hated that above all else. She pounded the pillow.

An image of him climbing into bed came to mind as clear as if he were next to her. That smile, oh, that smile! What would it be like to lie in his arms?

No, you fool, she told herself. He does not love you. You are a duty . . . and an ungrateful one at that.

Now tears of self-pity flowed. She had always been a duty to be discharged, and she wanted more. She mulled over her thoughts for a while, taking comfort in her self-pity. She wanted to find someone to love and be loved by—just like the Jenny she had once seen. The need for such a love was so real, it lay as a pain in her heart. She had understood that kind of caring though she had been young when she had seen the lovely pampered lady.

What silly schoolgirl dreams these were. She must divest herself of them. She was a woman now, a wife, and it was her duty to act like one. Since the age of eight she had managed to make life suit her, or at least find her niche.

She could do so now. She would go to London with Blanche and learn all there is to being a countess. She would learn to be the grandest countess in all England. Lord Grahame would not regret marrying her. She could fulfill her duty just as he had. Come hell or high water, she would do it.

"I shall have a dozen children for him," she said aloud.

Fifteen

Lord Grahame rode out early; he needed exercise and time alone to think. Warmer air moving into the valley brought rolling billows of fog, an accompanying stillness, and the promise of coming spring. It is odd how birds remain hushed in fog and before battle, he thought. It brought an eerie silence, as if they knew something you did not.

He picked his way carefully, because the ground was partially obscured. He wanted to race across the fields, but that would be foolhardy for both his mount and his neck.

Making his way on a trail that led to a hill several miles behind the lodge, he came out of the fog at the higher elevation. He paused at the summit and gazed out over the sea of pale gray fog. A soft breeze caressed his cheek, and the smell of the wet earth that heralds spring brought a response of exhilaration. He took a deep breath and let it out slowly to savor the feeling.

Overlooking the expanse, he remembered the many times he had sat his horse, viewing a field of soldiers. Shifting in his saddle to ease his bad leg, he thought of battle, the quiet, deadly silence before conflict. That ominous moment before the committing of his troops, when the outcome remained as shrouded as the valley before him. The instant when you sent a silent prayer to God that your decision was correct and your men fortified enough to deliver victory. The pervading silence recalled these memories with unnerving reality.

The terrible, ominous moment always passed, and he had signaled his army into action. In order to do so, he had thought of it in a collected term. He had never permitted himself to think in terms of boys and men about to die. He had to face that after the carnage, and then it was too horrible. But a commander must always think in terms of the army as a machine. He shook his head and let out another sigh that came from the depths of his being. Perhaps it was a blessing that his warrior days were over, he thought, and unconsciously rubbed his thigh.

The thought occurred to him that now, for the first time in his life, he was forced to think in terms of the individual. Eugenia was the responsibility he faced alone, and he did not know how to handle it.

To command hundreds he understood, but to take charge of one young lady and her future seemed totally outside his ability. A sadness descended, and he felt helpless. How could he guide her when he wasn't sure of their direction?

He was not sure of his feelings or motivations. He wanted to provide her with all that she needed, but he knew within his heart she needed little in the way of material advantage. Her greatest need was security of a home. That exigency he already met, but for how long would that be enough? Children would eventually fill the void of purpose, and he could give her them.

What of their needs? The need to be loved? He

had never felt the desire to marry; his military career had been his first and only love. The social pressure to wed and secure the line had never been paramount, but would have become so now that he had inherited his father's titles.

Fate had directed his choice, and it rankled. Despite all his efforts he could not help but resent the position in which he had been placed. True, he had accepted the solution, but would he have done them both a favor by refusing?

Eugenia had given him a refusal; he had his chance then. He wondered why he had not taken it. Like most of his peers, the hope for marriage based on love was not considered a necessity but happily embraced if fortunately found.

He liked Eugenia well enough. She is courageous, he thought, and he admired her for the very virtues he admired in men. She was intelligent and educated, he mused with a smile that changed his hard-set expression. Was it odd that he liked those attributes, when most men wanted a helpless mate with no thought of their own?

She is agreeable and eager to please, and he was also aware of her strong sense of justice, for he had seen her eyes flash with a crusader's fire. Realizing those virtues would be near impossible to find among the young ladies on the marriage mart, his smile widened.

He would hate to be saddled with a mealy-mouthed chit who would succumb to the vapors at the first sign of rough weather. Yes, he liked Eugenia's spirit. She had forged a life for herself in that drab school and offered her talents helping the equally lonely children. Yes, there was much to admire about his new wife. A voice within him whispered, Will that be enough? He could find no answer.

The image of her crossing the room on that cold day he had gone to fetch her came to his mind's eye. Such a drab little thing she had seemed. He remembered the helpless feeling that had flooded him. How would he find her a husband? he had wondered. She was far from the ladies he knew among the ton. He had realized that moment she would be eaten alive without his help and now, for the first time, recognized that motive.

She had crossed the room with her head bowed in trepidation. He remembered her trembling and his dismay. Then she had raised her eyes to him, looking directly into his and meeting him on equal ground. His heart skipped a little at the courage that had taken.

Her eyes! What gorgeous eyes! He could be lost in them forever. It was fun to rankle her, just to see them flare and change color. They seemed to defy him to seek the meaning behind them. What lay within her soul? He was drawn to the hidden mystery that hovered in flecks of green and gold-brown.

The memory of the shadow of her comely body revealed in the prim nightdress, which had stirred an ardor that had taken him by surprise, came to mind. The flame was not quenched, and he felt the heat of that desire still. Nature, he told himself. He acknowledged his amorous need and chastised himself, for herein lay the pitfall.

He must suppress his desire, which was based on the dictates of human nature. She was his wife, and a true gentleman did not take his wife like a common strumpet. They had a bargain, and he would respect it. This thought proved no comfort as he tugged at the reins to head back.

While the morning ride had given him time to mull over his situation, he found to his chagrin he had come to no conclusion. Damn, he thought, I am exactly where I was when I started out this morning.

He would treat her with respect and keep his distance. The trip to London would give her the experience and polish she needed to be a countess. He would not complicate that now. They could settle any change in the status of their marriage when he went up to join her. It is best we use this time to get to know each other. The foundations of their marriage would have to be laid carefully if they were to have any chance at success.

He knew he had his rights, but Eugenia needed time to adjust to the overwhelming changes in her life. He was not about to make a cake of himself by pressing his physical need of her, since it was only that and nothing else.

"Eugenia, the fog has cleared, and it's beautiful. Would you allow me to teach you to ride?"

She almost jumped with terror at his words. Her heart began to race. "My lord, I am terrified of horses. I do not think I could ever learn to ride."

"You managed to get on one when we left the cottage."

"That was a matter of life or death."

"I know it is best to learn to ride in childhood, but you could learn now. Many social events are designed to include riding."

"My lord, I want to do what you ask . . . but . . . I just could not get on the back of a horse."

"Have you ever tried? Not counting our escape, of course."

"Well, no . . ."

"Exactly my point. Allow me to teach you. I will be with you the whole time and promise not to push you."

Eugenia looked at the entreaty in his eyes. He wanted her to learn. She could not be so mean-spirited as not to at least try. "I suppose I can at least make an attempt."

"Good, then it is settled," he said, replacing his napkin on the table and rising.

"Let's go to the stables. I shall introduce you to the horses."

Her eyes widened, and her hand went slowly to her mouth.

"Do not look so stricken. I shall not sling you on one and send you racing off on your own."

She rose swiftly and forced a smile. "Yes, Lord Grahame, of course, you would not. I shall enjoy meeting the horses."

"You lie," he said, and laughed.

"I am encouraged by the fact that you recognized my deception." She smiled as their eyes met, nodded, and trailed after him as they left the dining room.

"I have no riding habit," she said with a glimmer of hope.

"Put on a warm cape and half-boots. We will try you with me and the cape will protect your modesty." He was enormously pleased as he gave her his instructions.

"Up with you? You mean *on* the horse?"

"Eugenia, get your cape."

* * *

Moments later they entered the stable. Eugenia was amazed at the luxurious interior. It must have cost as much as the house. Great Scot, she thought, they value their horses as much as they do themselves. That thought brought no comfort! She was bound to learn, trembly knees or no.

Grahame took her arm and gently drew her toward a stall. She slowed her steps, and his fingers tightened on her arm as her feet dragged behind. The gentle pull became a mild drag. She shuffled along, staying slightly behind his step.

A huge horse stood watching their approach. He snorted. Eugenia jumped, and slid behind Lord Grahame for protection. She peeked out from behind his back and stared at the monster, who had the temerity to stare back.

"He doesn't like me. I can tell. He is frowning at me. Let's go back."

Grahame chuckled. "He adores you. He is smiling in welcome."

She placed her hand on Grahame's arm and peeked around his back to look up into his face. Her eyes were wide in disbelief.

"You are funning me. How do you know what he is thinking?"

Grahame reached into a barrel and took a handful of oats. He took her hand and poured them into her palm. "Now, offer this to Fenrir in order to make friends."

"Fenrir! A wolf monster! You named him after a wolf monster? And you want me to feed *him* when his namesake was released to *eat* Odin?"

Grahame laughed as he brought his arm around her waist and drew her tight. "I shall protect you all the way."

With tiny tentative steps, and tucked in the strong arm of her husband, Eugenia moved forward. She raised her hand and opened her fist. Squeezing her eyes tight, she waited. A soft, warm mouth lightly brushed her skin. She opened her eyes and Fenrir was nibbling the oats in the gentlest manner possible. She stood fascinated. Fenrir raised his massive head and shook it. She smiled.

Grahame squeezed her waist tightly. "See, he is quite charmed by you."

Sixteen

Eugenia watched Grahame coming up the path from the stables. She stood at the window but far enough back to be out of his vision. The weather had held, the sun shone, and a high wind blew, which tousled his dark hair and whipped the skirt of his coat. The sight of him brought a thunder to her heart.

He carried himself with the superior military bearing of a soldier of the proud English Empire. His limp was slight and did not detract in any way. She knew he put great effort into walking with no evidence of his injury. Some days, she realized that effort was more bearable than others. It did seem as though he was less in pain than when she had first met him. She wanted to reach out to comfort him.

She could not read his expression, but it was thoughtful. What did he think of their beginning time together? She lacked any notion. He revealed nothing in his treatment of her. He behaved toward her as he might to any relative, never varying in his demeanor. Certainly there was no sense of intimacy or growing interest, merely a polite distance. Acceptance was the correct word; he accepted the situation.

The days had slipped by, and tomorrow they would leave for Windhaven. She smoothed her hair as she watched him disappear into the back entrance. Moving quickly to the chair set before the crackling fire, she picked up the book she had been trying to concentrate on and stared at the page. She would die if he knew she was watching him.

She had slipped into the pattern of behavior she came to understand was that of his lordship's. Since she had lacked any notion on how to act, she had allowed him to take the lead. Only once had she tried to seek an understanding of what he expected of her. She would never do that again!

Remembering the incident, she blushed. Her words came back to mind all too clear.

"Lord Grahame, I do want to uphold my end of the bargain," she had said the morning following their wedding. He had slept in the dressing room, and she had not been able to decide if it was by choice or because she had been so diffident. She suspected the latter.

In all honesty, she had to admit she had been less than welcoming to the idea of bedding with him. She shook her head and regretted the overt reluctance she had displayed. He was a proud man, and she could not tell what he thought, so she had made an effort to discuss it with him.

"I do not doubt you will," he had answered. She remembered wondering if there had been an amused interest in his demeanor. She suspected as much. The next words had been the hardest she had ever uttered.

"No, I mean . . . that is . . . I want to be all that you want me to be."

"None can be that, Eugenia. Not even those who

marry for love. If that is your ambition, you are doomed to failure."

She thought at the time the answer was caustic, but she now realized he had spoken the truth.

"My lord, you quite understand what I am attempting to say," she had said, pressing the point.

Eugenia's heart flipped now just as it had then, when he had leveled his icy eyes on her and waited one terrible silent moment before answering.

"We have already discussed this. We agreed that you would go to London with Blanche. You should have the opportunity of pretty gowns and the pleasure of balls. All young ladies look forward to this time in their lives. You should experience them. Ladies seem to hold great store by them."

"I do not look forward to London. I would be happier at Windhaven. I do not think society holds any interest for me nor I them."

"You will need to acquire the necessary town skills to carry out your duties. What better way than to experience them? I do not doubt your ability to do so with the utmost ease. You are quick-witted."

"But you said yourself you do not care for the round of social activities. I have heard you say they are a dead bore," she had countered.

"Ah, Madam Wife, I see you already tell me what I think. Do not overlook the fact I shall take my seat in Parliament and you will have need of the ways of the ton. There will be times when we must participate. Besides, I do not see how you can categorically decide you do not like something before you have experienced it." There had been some hidden reference in his words, or at least she thought so.

"What if I am not a credit to you?" She had said the fearful words in a voice little more than a whisper.

"Is that important?"

"My lord, of course it is! I wish you had a beautiful and clever wife. You deserve one, and I certainly do not make that mark!" She knew her words had been tinged with bitterness.

Lord Grahame was momentarily taken aback by the passion of her voice. "That is exactly why you should go. You will be there ahead of the onslaught of the eager beau ton. *Onslaught* is the correct word." He smiled, and crinkle lines appeared with twinkling eyes.

"You will meet fortune seekers, matchmaking mamas, libertines, and the socially ambitious. There will be a crush of people, all eager to make their mark, and the elevated few who pass judgment with a mere nod or cut that proves to be the social death for some poor victims."

Eugenia met his eyes. "That is what I fear most."

A flicker crossed his eyes, and he started to reach out his hand but let it drop by his side. "That is precisely why you should go. You will also meet kindness and those who will help you along."

She remained silent.

"I have engaged a dancing master for you. Blanche will see you turned out to the nines. And lest I make too much of my position, you are the Countess of Grahame, whose husband is a national war hero. Now, that should give you a certain position from which to look down your pretty nose on those with lesser titles."

"You are teasing! You know perfectly well I do not wish to look down on anyone any more than you do. I am sure that is equally abhorrent to you. I quite imagine it is exactly why you avoid the environs of society."

"Good, I am glad you see it thus. We find another area of compatibility." He sat back in the chair and hesitated a moment. "I think, however, there is another question that you are asking me. We also agreed to fill my . . . our . . . nursery when the time came. We both decided that was what we wanted. Have you changed your mind on this aspect of our situation?"

Eugenia shivered with the memory of the flash of fire that flickered ever so briefly deep within his silver eyes. He had waited quietly for her answer. There had been an underlying tension she had not felt before. Lord, how she now regretted ever bringing up the topic!

"It was reassurance, my lord, which led me to broach the subject. I shall not do so again."

"Good, then it is again settled." The memory of his knowing glance and disarming smile sent shivers down her spine once more. She buried her face in her hands—how utterly embarrassing that moment had been!

Eugenia forced her thoughts back to the present and listened for his footsteps. She could not hear his coming to her and sat back with relief. It will be easier, she thought, when we are not isolated with only each other to find diversion. Thank God, he had planned only one week alone.

There had been times of pure enjoyment. He could be great company, but she doubted he felt that way about her. She had nothing to base that idea on; it was her assumption. They had read to each other, played cards and chess in the evenings with affable ease.

The most outstanding endeavor of the week had been his getting her on that brute of a horse, even if it had been brief. She smiled at the memory. Was not it odd, how she could remember every minute detail when they had been together. She knew every move, expression, and word he had uttered.

She supposed it was her extraordinary care to behave in the best possible manner. She tried to be agreeable every moment, and the strain was frightfully wearing. She suspected it made him uncomfortable, and so she tried all the harder. "London begins to look like a promising relief," she said aloud to the empty room and herself.

His mighty stallion would put anyone to fright, she mused as she continued to remember the incident. The day following her first venture into the stables, Grahame had insisted they try again. Off they had gone, with what she assumed was Lord Grahame's optimistic idea that he was about to turn his mouse of a wife into a fearless horsewoman. She remembered almost fainting when the groom had brought out the saddled, snorting beast.

"I hope he doesn't think I am Odin," she said in an effort to be amusing.

"If he does, I shall avenge you by being your Vidar."

"My lord, that is no comfort," she replied in mock horror.

He chuckled, and she remembered feeling happy she had made him laugh.

She remembered watching him swing up into the saddle and motion to the groom to help her up in front of him. The moment was the worst of her entire life; she had to obey. She had disappointed him before, and now they were all standing there watching. Oh, she could smile now, but then, she had been about to expire on the spot.

Seated in front of him, he set the horse into a slow walk. She had not been able to control her trembling, and he tightened his arm arou

er in quick response. He held her tightly as they moved out into the courtyard. His strong arm and solid body offered security, but fear continued to rack her body.

"I'll not let you fall," he whispered in her ear.

She remembered his breath and lips so close to her ear and the tingle that ran through her body. The memory brought a flood of color to her cheeks as it had each time she recalled the incident, the many times she had lain alone in bed with the image of his embrace that had forced her to relive the overwhelming emotion of his nearness. That emotion was both pleasure and pain.

She refused to examine the reason and did not do so now. She dismissed it as a natural reaction to an attractive male. But despite her dismissal, it was so disturbing, she could not help returning to it repeatedly.

She snapped the book shut. Enough of these foolish thoughts! She was doing the best she could, and that would have to be good enough. Lord Grahame seemed to take all the events of the week in his stride. She doubted whether he spent agonizing hours mulling over the least little detail of everything said and done. It was foolish of her to do so. She squared her shoulders with the thought that the past is the past and the future would take care of itself. "Brave words," she muttered, and giggled.

"Your ladyship, may we come in to set up for the evening meal?" Mrs. Beekans asked as she entered the room.

"But of course. The afternoon has slipped away. I believe the peace of this house could become a favorite haven," Eugenia replied.

"Aye, 'tis a lovely place. We hope all has been to your satisfaction. We look forward to you coming again soon. It is a pleasure when we have something to do," Mrs. Beekans said as she began to arrange the table.

"It has been a lovely time. I shall hate to leave tomorrow," Eugenia said as she hurried to go to change. If only I could stay forever, Eugenia thought, and never have to face all the unknowns of the Season in London.

Seventeen

The flames flared and danced with scattering sparks when Thomas added more logs to the fire. He replaced the fire tongs with his usual swift, sure movements, but there was about him an undeniable tension or restraint. Turning to Eugenia, who had taken a seat in the high wing chair, his expression changed little, but he spoke with an effort to be cheerful.

"Let's enjoy the fire awhile. I'm convinced the dampness of early spring is more pervading than the bite of winter." Moving to the table that held the crystal decanter and glasses, he removed the stopper. "A bit of brandy?"

"Yes, a small amount, please. It can warm my veins as the fire does my toes," she answered while stretching her feet to the fireplace. She suspected she was feeling the same finality to this evening as her husband. Tomorrow they were to go to London. The thought brought apprehension in a skip of her heart and dryness to her mouth.

He handed her a glass and took the chair opposite her before the hearth. Raising his glass, he said, "To the future."

She raised her glass in response. "Whatever that may hold."

Grahame nodded, then took a sip. "Ah, the unknown, pesky though it may be."

"Pesky?" she asked.

He raised an eyebrow in mock surprise. "Of course, the future is always troublesome by virtue of the simple fact that it is unknown. Don't you agree the possibility of not having control over what is to come brings a certain sense of misgiving, even fear?"

"My lord, we all have the control of how we address this unknown. You would have to agree with that. We do have a choice."

"Now, Eugenia, you tread into the prerogatives of the philosophers on fate and free will. Despite your brave words, surely you dread the expedition of going to London and facing the intricacies of the Season?"

She felt her heart thumping again. If only he knew how terrified she was. "Hmm, yes, but I am trying to present an air of unconcern." She wanted to add that it was not easy, but she had spoken with enough frankness and, besides, it would sound self-serving. She waited for his response with interest.

He chuckled. "If you manage a facade of unconcern, you have already learned all you need to know in negotiating the harrows of the Season. To appear too eager would be tantamount to the cardinal sin of the ton. One must strive to appear uninterested, and at best merely slightly amused. The slightly is very important."

"You are teasing, of course, yet I think you are dead serious." Silently, she scoffed at the idea of acting indifferent as anything new to her. It had been the only way she had survived.

"Astute pupil! You will do well. I have known

from the first: You had the makings of an admirable countess."

Eugenia's cheeks flushed with embarrassment at his high praise. "Your compliment is far too extravagant. You knew no such thing." She could not believe in his words when she felt like an intruder, an impostor, and she hated it.

"Ah, you see you have passed the second test! You will be inundated with specious compliments, all to be taken with the equally modest denial that somehow bespeaks the fact that they are duly deserved."

Eugenia forced a laugh. Deep within she knew she could never muster such arrogance. Where would it come from?

"You exaggerate, of course," she said.

He feigned a hurt expression. "Eugenia!" he said, placing his hand over his heart. "I swear it is the truth. The compliments will flow with such adulation you will be forced to turn around to see if the gallant is speaking to you or to someone standing behind you."

Now, *that* she could believe. She knew she wasn't pretty and had never had reason to consider it before, nor had she cared.

"How does one respond?"

"As I have said, in modest denial that somehow implies it is justly deserved."

"My, my, I'm not sure I can manage that."

"You will, just try not to laugh. Unless, of course, it is a titter. Titters are acceptable."

"Oh, how dreadful! Can you imagine me tittering?"

"Frankly, no, you'll have to depend on the regal nod of acceptance, or perhaps a blushing, modest denial. There is always the faraway-bored look, but somehow I think that is unkind. After all, some of these dandies spend hours before their mirrors practicing the polished phrases."

"I will remember that, and treat those studied utterances with due respect. I can't imagine you delivering effusive compliments."

He raised an eyebrow in mock surprise. "You can't? You are wrong. However, I do admit to making them nearest the truth as possible."

She giggled. "I cannot wait."

"To receive the compliments?"

"No, to see you bowed over some damsel's hand, offering outrageous flattery."

"You will wait for that. I leave London to you and Blanche. I shall join you later, but I am not one to enjoy drawing-room dawdle."

"I am afraid I shall hate it," she said, and raised her chin in slight defiance.

"It is my experience, the ladies thrive on it."

"It seems to me, my lord, the gentlemen must enjoy the game or they would not play at it. Men generally manage to arrange their pastimes to suit their desires. I quite imagine, in many instances, there is something they wish to gain from such flowery speech."

"What could they possibly gain other than a reputation for being gallant?"

"Someone's bed, I should imagine."

Brandy sprayed out in a choking cough. Lord Grahame had been in the midst of a swallow when Eugenia stated the obvious. It took several seconds to control the coughing fit, for it had turned into laughter.

"Now, that will never do! Suddenly, I am overwhelmed by a sense of foreboding. Kindly keep such truthful thoughts to yourself when mingling with the ever-so-proper aristocracy. They do not care what you do, just do not mention it or flaunt it," he said, still laughing. "Eugenia, you are always a surprise."

"Is that one of those compliments?" she teased.

"From me, yes. Just do not try such cleverness in a drawing room."

The laughter died. They sat quietly, staring at the fire. Eugenia regretted her impertinent answer. She had gone too far. Should she apologize?

"My lord . . ."

"Eugenia, my name is Thomas."

"Thomas, I apologize. I should never have said that. I was teasing. It was such fun."

"Eugenia, I enjoyed the conversation, too! You may say whatever you wish to me. You spoke only the truth, but you have never been in the august salons of the beau ton. London society is in for a surprise, I fear," he said, and laughed again.

"It might be worth coming with you just to see how you get on."

"I shall be most discreet."

"You may be surprised, but I don't doubt that for a minute. My best advice is to think before you speak and never mention people getting into beds other than their own. Thank God, you will have Blanche at your side, and she knows far more than I do."

"I doubt that, Thomas! I shall be at a total loss without you. How will I ever manage?" she said, batting her eyelashes at him.

"Why, Eugenia, are you flirting with me?"

"Heavens no. I don't even know how!"

"Hmmm, well, we shall let Blanche teach you the art of flirting."

"I have no intention of learning. Why would I want to?"

Grahame looked at her and smiled but refrained from answering.

Silence once more fell between them. A few moments later Lord Grahame rose. "Come, it is late. Tomorrow we leave early."

Eugenia had just taken down her hair and picked up her brush when Grahame entered from the adjoining dressing room. She began to brush her hair while she watched him in the mirror. He crossed the room, stood behind her, and lightly placed his hand on her shoulder.

Their eyes met in the reflection. "I think we have managed well. Do you agree?" he asked.

Replacing the brush, she rose and moved around the chair to stand before him. "I agree, and I am glad for the opportunity to thank you."

He raised an eyebrow in a questioning gesture.

"You have been most kind . . . I . . . am . . ." Her words faded in the spellbinding emotion that passed between them. Her heart responded wildly to the passionate flame in his eyes.

Slowly his hand came up and he slipped it around her waist. Gently drawing her to him, he lowered his mouth to hers and gave her a gentle brush of his lips. "Kindness has nothing to do with it," he said, and tightened his hold.

She raised her hands to his chest and started to step back, but his embrace tightened and he lowered his lips to hers again. His kiss was at first cautious, tenuous, then became more sure and encompassing. His arms pulled her into his strong, masculine body. At first she tried to pull apart but found, instead, her arms moving up and around his neck.

He kissed her repeatedly. His lips moved to her eyes, her cheeks, and back to her waiting mouth. All time and thought slipped from her mind, and she trembled with the trilling, electrifying tremor that surged through her body. He lifted his head a moment and looked into her eyes. He slowly untied the belt to her velvet robe and slipped the garment from her shoulders. It fell to the floor in a pool at her feet.

He touched her flowing hair and ran his fingers along her cheek. She stood transfixed, unable to move or think. He bent to kiss her again. His lips traveled down her neck as he lifted her in his arms. Her head rested against his chest, and she could hear his heart beating as fast as hers. Or was it only hers she heard?

His strong arms held her close as he carried her to the bed. His lips sought her mouth again. He placed her on the bed, never letting her go.

"Eugenia," he murmured, and the rest of his words were lost to the probing kiss.

Her arms went around him, and she drew him to her. She wanted him to hold her and kiss her. Never had she felt so alive and enraptured. She waited with tingling anticipation for his touch.

His fingers untied the ribbons that held her nightdress closed, and then slid along her waist. He raised his head and looked again into her eyes. He could see the warm glow of passion that encouraged him.

Rolling off the bed, he blew out the candles, and

by the firelight she could see him remove his robe and nightshirt. He stood a second, looking at her, waiting for her refusal or invitation.

She raised her arms to him, and he drew back the covers for them both. Sliding in next to her, he drew her back into his arms. She could feel the strong muscles of his arms and chest as she embraced him. She was swept up in the power of him—his taste, his smell, and his passion.

"Sweet Eugenia," he murmured as his hand slid along her smooth skin.

His touch brought a response that both thrilled and surprised her, and she waited, desiring every caress. She returned his probing kisses and held him closer. He was delighted at the sweet response of his wife.

His touch was gentle, and he wooed her with each step he took into the journey of lovemaking. He kissed her and whispered that she was beautiful, and her reason for being answered each caress.

"I had thought to wait, but I need you now," he said, pulling her even closer.

Eighteen

"My pardon for waking you so early, my lady," Mrs. Beekans said with a contrite glance that went unseen by her sleeping mistress. "I hope you slept well," she continued as she placed a tray on the table.

The tempting smell of hot chocolate and fresh bread reached Eugenia's nostrils, stirring her senses as she tried to rouse her body and mind. The instigated awakening came as a rude shock, and she sought to get her bearings. It was a struggle, for she came from a deep, profound sleep.

"I'll send up your bathwater as soon as you are finished. Is there anything else I can do for you?"

"No, thank you. I didn't realize it was so late. I'll hurry," Eugenia muttered, still trying to shake the fog from her mind.

"Lord Grahame says to take your time, but he'd like an early start," Mrs. Beekans said with a curtsy, then departed.

Lord Grahame! Eugenia's mind snapped into the present. Her heart quivered as her hand strayed from the warmth of the covers to the empty spot where he had lain the previous night. She withdrew her hand as quickly, for the coldness of the bed linen and emptiness of the space reached her heart with crushing dismay. Why had not he awakened her in the morning instead of sending a servant to tell her it was time to prepare to leave? She blushed and buried her head in her pillow. She thought he would be beside her to waken her with kisses. Had she disappointed him?

She didn't understand the subtleties in married life, or anything else, for that matter. Apparently, she should not expect tender, solicitous treatment. Why this reaction? Was she placing some fault on his part for not being by her side with an enamored expression? She fought back tears.

How very foolish! This was not a love marriage. He had married her to defend her honor. Yet his lovemaking had seemed like all that love could be, and she had taken it as such. That was a witless mistake. What a green goose she was!

She had been warned by grave-faced teachers that men had certain desires, and it was well to remember their words. Why else would families watch their daughters with eagle eyes?

He had merely taken what he had the right to, and he had been kind and gentle. What was her complaint? She should be grateful; he might have been some brute. All her life she had had to accept what men decreed; why should she expect anything different? She must remember she did not live in a fairy tale!

She threw back the covers with a determined stroke. It would be simple enough to put on a pleasant face and harbor no calf-moon expectations. The much-loved "Jenny" was a figment of an adolescent mind; she would do well to remember that.

* * *

When she reached the bottom of the stairway she was still annoyed at the racing of her heart. She could muster a pragmatic expression and viewpoint, but her heart refused to obey. She was bound to be dead of some weakened condition before she was twenty-two if she could not still her wayward organ. To go through life with a pounding heart every time she was in proximity of her husband was not her idea of control. Her hand touched her midriff as if to restrain her emotions.

Just as she reached the entrance hall Lord Grahame entered dressed in his riding clothes. Her first response when their eyes met was to think he looked tired. She managed a smile.

"Good morning, my lord. Surely, I have not kept you waiting too long?"

"Good morning, Eugenia. No, I'm delighted to find my wife is prompt. I consider myself to be twice fortunate. You slept well, I trust?"

Bully for you, she thought, and a slow indignation rose. *The patronizing fool* fit neatly in her mind as she clenched her fists. She had the strongest desire to stick her tongue out at him. The urge was overwhelming, and it was her years of discipline in hiding her emotions that allowed her to overcome the tempting inclination. Realizing the impotency of this childish reaction, she drew herself up and squared her shoulders.

"Quite well, thank you," she replied in the same honeyed, false inflection she seemed to read in him.

"Good, then we'd best be off," he said, opening the door and gesturing for her to precede him.

She sailed past in what she hoped was a regal manner. She did not see the smile that fluttered across his eyes and twitched his lips.

His hand caught her arm, and he guided her to the waiting coach. Footmen were busy securing the luggage, and the coachman had mounted the box. Eugenia noticed his lordship's fine stallion saddled and waiting. He intended riding outside, and she was grateful for that! She glanced at him but saw no discernible expression.

Assisting her into the coach, he adjusted the lap robe. "There, are you comfortable?" he asked.

"Quite," she replied, and turned to look out the opposite window.

Grahame stood a moment as if wanting to say something, then turned and nodded to the footman to raise the steps. He mounted his stallion and let out a breath. He had gotten it all wrong; he knew *that* without a doubt! But he hadn't known what to say to her. He had displayed pure cowardice. He shrugged. How should he have handled the situation? He had used every method of seduction he knew last evening. He had wanted her, plain and simple. Now he was ashamed. His motive had not been very noble in the light of their agreement of a marriage of convenience.

Justifying his actions by the fact that it was his right to take his wife to himself was no consolation. He had not been considerate of her feelings. She had been so warm and wonderful in his arms. The warmth of her embraces still lingered. Damn, he didn't know how to get on in an arranged marriage! He kneed his horse into a gallop.

The coach and six moved out behind him with a sudden start. Eugenia bounced in response. It is going to be a long journey, she thought with a frown, and she wasn't referring to the trip only.

* * *

They reached London from the west and entered Manchester Square before sunset. Eugenia was tired and relieved to make their destination before nightfall. The coach pulled into the square and stopped before an imposing Italianate house.

The entrance had an arched loggia, which survived as the load-bearing structure for the four Corinthian columns that rose to an unadorned entablature and pediment. The house was of Portland stone and the corners completed the harmony of the design with Corinthian capped pilasters. The brilliant design was taken from the villas of Florence and sat comfortably among other grand houses of the square.

The large door opened and a footman rushed forward to help the travelers. Lord Grahame had moved swiftly to the door of the carriage, and as soon as the steps were let down, he offered his hand to Eugenia.

She took his proffered hand and momentarily searched his face for some expression. He offered a slight smile that could probably be termed a society smile, and it rankled her. Just like some acquaintance! She returned the insipid smile and lifted her chin.

From the covered entrance she could not examine the house, but her curiosity was distracted when Blanche emerged from the doorway to welcome them. Blanche rushed to embrace them both and chatted on about being utterly bored, awaiting their arrival.

They hurried into the great hall with its famous curved stairway, and everyone began to speak at once.

"I have ordered a hot bath for you. I know you

are tired. Come, I shall show you to your rooms." Blanche noted with interest Eugenia's pinched look. She could not decide if it was fatigue or that things had not gone well. She glanced over to her brother. Their eyes met, and he smiled and gave her a slight nod. She wasn't sure what he meant, but it was obvious he was not tired or distressed. Good.

She took Eugenia's arm and they mounted the steps to the first floor and the earl's apartments.

"The bedrooms face the garden, not the street, although our square is not often noisy. The sitting room is situated between both your bedrooms. It is very pleasant indeed." Blanche opened the door to the large sitting room.

Eugenia caught her breath. The room was large and exquisite. High ceilings were cast-plastered in patterns of large squares edged in vines and leaves. In the center of the squares large paterae carried the same motif, creating an effect of delicacy and refinement.

The brocade fabrics were jewel-colored, deep ruby, purple, and green blended beautifully against the white walls and wainscoting. The furniture was the very latest, in classical design brought into fashion by Napoleon's adventures.

"It is amazing how much we hate the French and are at war with them every few years, yet we ape their design," Blanche said with a chuckle as she watched Eugenia's eyes scan the room.

"Blanche, it is beautiful!"

"Come, allow me to show you your bedchambers."

Eugenia's bedchamber was off to the right, and she trailed Blanche into what was to be her sanctuary while in London.

"There is a small sitting room through this door for your use. It gets the morning sun and is the perfect place for your correspondence, reading, or taking tea with special friends."

Her rooms were the same jewel colors. Jardiniere velvets were used to add multicolored patterns resembling a flower grouping against a light ground. Persian carpets carried the color in harmony to the floor. It was breathtaking, and Eugenia stood speechless. How could she be comfortable here? It was too elegant!

Eugenia divested herself of her bonnet and gloves. She removed her cape and a hovering maid took the clothing from her hands. Eugenia looked up at the eager face of the waiting maid and smiled. The maid seemed relieved. Great Scot, the maid is fearful of meeting me, she thought. I have more to get used to than I care to. "Blanche, how do you tolerate all these servants?"

Blanche laughed as she gave instructions to the footman bringing water to the large tub set by the fire.

"We have to. There is no other choice. We could not live as we do without help. It would be impossible," Blanche said, waving her jewel-covered fingers in fluttering helplessness.

Eugenia laughed. "I may even come to agree, but you must understand, it does take some getting accustomed to! I loved the hunting box for the very reason there were few servants. I fear I am quite plebeian."

Blanche laughed and waved her hand to the maid who held Eugenia's cloak and bonnet. "Eugenia, this is Maggie. She is to be your abigail. She does wonders with a needle and will see to your clothes and hair. Maggie, this is your new mistress, the Countess of Grahame."

Eugenia's heart gave a lurch at hearing her title, but she smiled to the girl who was delivering a curtsy. Eugenia realized she was again given a maid of little hauteur and silently blessed Blanche's insight.

"I am pleased to have you assist me," Eugenia kindly said, and was rewarded with a smiling face.

"I have taken the liberty of having a few things placed in your wardrobe, but tomorrow we begin in earnest to properly outfit you. What delicious fun. Tonight, however, we shall dine early *en famille* so you can get to bed early. I know the journey was tiring, and you will need all your strength for shopping." Blanche clapped her hands to dismiss the servants who had brought in the bathtub, and moved to leave.

Maggie returned from putting Eugenia's outer garments away. She carried a gown of muslin trimmed at the sleeves and neck with apricot rushing. "Would this be your choice for dinner?" Maggie asked.

Eugenia had never seen the dress before, but nodded dumbly. Another dress from Blanche, she thought. Gracious, the woman was daft to think she needed so many gowns.

As Maggie put up the screen, Eugenia slipped out of her dress, pausing before stepping out of her chemise and petticoat. She hated the idea of having someone help her bathe. She blushed at the intrusion, wondering how and if ever she would get used to having a servant hovering about. It was positively creepy. She stepped into the water and slid down. The warmth was soothing and she closed her eyes. The idea of "Jenny" definitely had its drawbacks.

Nineteen

Lord Grahame entered his wife's bedchamber early the next morning. Eugenia was awake and about to rise to face the day of shopping Blanche had promised. She had lingered as long as she dared because the bed was so inviting. She blushed at his entrance.

"Good morning, Eugenia, I have come to bid you farewell. I leave you to the damage Blanche can create in the mantua-makers and bonnet shops of London." He chuckled.

"My lord, Blanche's ideas far exceed my own. I have more than I need now." She was still embarrassed by the magnitude of the possessions being offered and more embarrassed by her defensive denials. They sounded self-serving as she listened to herself placing the fault at Blanche's doorstep, and blushed deeper. She was trying to make Thomas understand she did not want his money, and she had done so at Blanche's expense. What a coward she was. And Blanche was so kind to her. She did not feel like a countess, she felt like an impostor.

"Eugenia, I have promised to turn you into 'Jenny,' and so I shall. It is my pleasure, I assure you. So you must throw yourself into the venture with unabashed pleasure. I shall be disappointed if

I am not able to complain to my peers of the burdens of a wife gone mad in the shops along Bond Street. You would not deprive me of that pleasure, would you?"

She giggled and slipped lower in the covers. "I shall try to exceed your wishes. May I also purchase some of the latest books?"

He placed his hand on the bedpost and gave her an intimate, devastating smile. He was pleased with her answer.

"Mr. Hartwell, my man of business, is to call today. I have instructed him to give you a quarterly allowance that you will be challenged to spend. You may buy all that you wish. Blanche will show you the jewelry that is now yours, as you may wish to reset some or match frocks and gowns to others."

A frown fluttered across her face. "I am not sure . . . jewels . . ." She sat up and gathered her thoughts. "This is all too much for me. I do not mean to sound ungrateful, but there it is . . . the truth."

"Eugenia, your feelings on this do not disappoint me. However, you must remember you are the Countess of Grahame and so must appear. The title takes certain responsibilities, and among those is looking absolutely outstanding."

"Now you do frighten me!"

"You will get used to the idea. Luxury has a way of doing that. What seems like an extravagance will soon become a necessity. I will be back to London for your Court presentation and to squire my stunning wife about town. Learn all Blanche has to teach. You see, I take a coward's role and head for cover at Windhaven." He bent down and placed a kiss on her forehead. "I will be back before a fortnight. Good luck."

He was amused as he left the room. She remained still several moments, staring at the closed door through which he had passed. How was she going to divorce her growing love for him from the life she would spend with him?

It was hard to tell what he thought. He had not come to her bed since the last evening of their stay at the hunting box. She was sure she had disappointed him in some way. What could she have done differently? She quickly drove that thought from her mind. It hurt too much.

Still, she could not deny he seemed pleased. His eyes had twinkled, and he seemed amused at the idea of turning her into a lady of fashion. God forbid, she did not even know whether she wanted to be one anymore. The fascination of the "Jenny" she had seen was beginning to lose its appeal. Perhaps "epitome" was far better left in a daydream than found in reality.

She could not imagine herself all decked out in jewels. Suddenly, the idea became amusing. Maybe that is how he sees me! She surprised herself by thinking it equally humorous instead of adding some failing on her part. Perhaps the transformation has begun, she thought, enormously pleased at the idea.

True to Blanche's vows, the famous, or infamous, depending how one looks at this sort of thing, Henri appeared with bustling attendant and snapping scissors. Blanche stood by, supervising every snip.

Eugenia sat meekly, staring at her reflection, while they talked about her in the third person.

The slender Henri sported a thin mustache, flamboyant gestures, and a fake French accent. She was so taken with the scene being played out before her, she remained detached and completely entertained.

She had so turned herself over to their ministrations, she failed to get alarmed when sheaves of hair began falling. She listened to his "zis and zat, ma assez, madame," until she could hardly suppress a smile. Her head was pushed this way and that as curling irons forced her mass of hair into submission.

"Now, what does her ladyship think?" Henri said with a flourish that brought her attention to her reflection.

She gasped. Her heart-shaped face stared back with a mass of curls tousled in planned disarray. Pounds of hair seemed to be gone, and she felt both light-headed and lighthearted. The coiffure completely changed her looks. Gone was the severe style, and in its place was a transforming miracle.

"You have underrated your talents, monsieur," she said in a disbelieving voice.

"Eugenia, you look enchanting! I knew it." Blanche clapped her hands. "Now, Maggie, did you see just how it is done?"

Maggie nodded mutely, fervently hoping she could manage as well. "I am sure I will be able to do so. It is in the cut."

"But of course!" Henri said, bowing in all modesty.

No time was wasted. Eugenia felt pommeled and plummeted, talked above, below, and about. Fabrics appeared, disappeared in moments; laces, trims, beads, and feathers marched before her eyes. Her head whirled, and she soon gave up any attempt at exclaiming: enough!

Blanche knew very well what she was doing and brought to the fore her powers to turn out a well-dressed lady. Carriage dresses, walking dresses, a Court dress, riding habits, morning gowns, and ball gowns claimed time for attention.

Next they visited several milliners to choose just this bonnet with that color, matched to perfection from a slip of fabric. Gloves, shoes, fans, and an array of unmentionables, stockings, and night-gowns were ordered by the dozens.

"Blanche! I quit thinking hours ago. My feet hurt, my head hurts, and I am hungry. Not a step farther. I rebel."

"Oh, my. I am sorry, dear. We can finish later. Yes, let us go. We must have a bite to eat. You will rest so we can attend the opera tonight."

"If I have the fortitude, Blanche. You amaze me."

"I have three daughters, who, by the way, are expecting a little gift when we return. We must choose something quickly."

Eugenia wilted. "Hurry!"

Blanche laughed.

Eugenia's education began in earnest the following morning. She spent an hour with the assigned dancing master and another with Blanche, learning how to enter a room, take a seat, and make a very proper curtsy. These endeavors were new to Eugenia, and she found herself enjoying the tasks. She especially liked the dancing. Her progress was such, she suspected, she would actually be able to take to the dance floor in the future. She hoped it would be with Thomas.

The thought of him brought a catch to her heart. She prayed madly that he would be pleased with her progress when he arrived. In the same breath she prayed she would not have to face him soon.

Blanche took her on calls to various friends, and she was grandly received. Not being obtuse, Eugenia knew it was her title they were receiving. She felt speculative glances over her sudden marriage to the earl, and could not decide if they were real or in her imagination.

Somehow she managed to abide these visits with a certain resignation—even humor. This attitude translated into a casual air that in turn was perceived as confidence by those who met her. Eugenia was unaware of this, but it was to her advantage.

When her name came up in conversations over tea, it was declared that she was a well-turned-out young lady. Blanche was aware of her small success and breathed a sigh of relief. Thomas would be grateful, and she was, too. She had become very fond of Eugenia.

Eugenia's first evening entertainment was the opera. Madame Catalani, who had not appeared in London for three years, was singing. When they arrived they found the lane crowded with carriages. London had turned out en masse to hear the beautiful Italian sing.

Eugenia was awed by the many tiered boxes where the wealthy paid as much as 2,500 pounds for a subscription. They sat on comfortable chairs while the general audience sat on benches.

Madame Catalani had a lovely voice, and Eugenia was enchanted. She sat in wonder at the sight and sounds and more than once wished Thomas were there to enjoy the performance. See, she was doing it again. Thomas this, Thomas that. She simply had to put her husband out of her mind.

On the trip home Eugenia watched the flickering lanterns casting small pools of light onto the streets and walks. London was a hodgepodge of humanity. One minute they stood beside well-dressed ladies covered with jewels. Along the street walked shabbily dressed people going in all directions. Occasionally one could see a drunk weaving along the walkway.

She spied a little girl trying to sell a few apples. Her heart gave a lurch. The child should be in bed. Suddenly, loneliness swept her. Tears stung. She thought of the children at the school. How unfair life could be. She missed them, yet she had hardly given them a thought these past weeks. Had she so changed? God forbid, she thought. Would she become one of those who ignored the ills of the less fortunate? It was easy to drift along in the life being placed before her. The new sights, sounds, and luxuries were certainly exciting, and she was enjoying all she was learning.

But deep down she would never be one of "them," and yet she could never go back to who she had been. Was she forever to be between two worlds? She had made a niche for herself before; could she do so again? She doubted it, for this time she had to please others. Therein lay the pitfall. Could she please her husband? If she managed the transfer to his world, would she please herself? What a mess, and she had no answer.

Eugenia was beyond tired when they reached the town house and more than a little discouraged by her thoughts and the blame she put on herself and her perceived failings.

Blanche was all smiles and bid Eugenia good night. "Tomorrow evening we attend the Marquis of Salisbury's party. So hurry to bed and do sleep in come morning. I think your new gown trimmed with green velvet banding will be the thing."

Eugenia bid Lloyd and Blanche good night. She headed to bed with a growing dismay. There would be dancing tomorrow evening, and she had not yet tried it in public. Oh, why couldn't she have stayed at Windhaven with Thomas? She felt a shudder. Tears threatened. That is all I need, she thought, to feel sorry for myself when all the world is being offered to me. But the world was Thomas, and he was now and had always been beyond her reach. She fell asleep crying.

Twenty

"Why do you stand alone, half hidden by a potted fern?"

Eugenia started at the voice that interrupted her musing. She turned to face a tall, impeccably dressed man. He was not handsome but emitted a compelling appeal. It was his eyes that held the intriguing quality. She was not sure but suspected it to be some irony, but not without humor. Responding to that humor, she sent a smile that lit her face and danced in her eyes.

"You must admit, sir, the scene before us hovers on absurdity, yet offers an undeniable fascination. The study of the people is irresistible, and what place better to observe them than behind a potted plant?"

The gentleman lifted his quizzing glass and studied the throng for a moment. "I am persuaded to agree. It surprises me that I become so accustomed to such a crush; it is taken as commonplace. It is refreshing to see it from new eyes."

Eugenia laughed. An affinity sprang up between them, and she responded by revealing her thoughts. "I suspect the study of human behavior is always fascinating. It is easy to miss what is around us when we become too interested ourselves. When that happens, I also suspect a certain flatness must come to our lives. To observe others is infinitely entertaining."

He studied her a moment. Odd little thing, he thought. She was no beauty. Still, there was an irresistible quality to her. She was beautifully dressed in a slender, understated gown that was suited uniquely to her. Her hair, a mass of curls, tied with a band of green velvet, framed her face.

He approved of her style, and to him that denoted intelligence. Style was the mark of a gentleman or lady. A spark of life emanated from her beautiful eyes, and her sensuous mouth smiled with a bit of irony. He had been curious about her from afar, but now became remarkably interested in her.

"You are new to London?"

"Yes, I am. . . ."

"No, do not tell me. First, tell me what you see in this melee. Your opinion would be colored if I knew who you are. We can make our introductions later."

Eugenia laughed and turned her face to the dancing couples and the milling guests crowded along the edges of the ballroom. He liked the silvery ring of her laugh and the honesty it held. There was no missish giggle, and only the Lord knew how many of those he had had to bear.

"I see much laughter but not much happiness, I fear," she said, taken by his interest and falling into the rhythm of his thought.

He lifted his quizzing glass again, scanned the smiling faces of the ton. "I find myself in complete agreement. You must consider, however, they seek diversion, not happiness," he said, and turned to rest his eyes on her.

"No, my lord, they seek happiness in diversion. I suspect it is seldom found there."

"Indeed? And how would you know?"

"Everyone seeks happiness, my lord. The problem, I think, is that most people do not recognize it."

"I concede the point. You are correct. Where do you think happiness can be found?"

"I am not sure myself. Perhaps in service or acceptance, but never in unending rounds of parties. I do know one cannot pursue it, yet it will not come if one sits and waits." She laughed and turned to him. "I quite surprise myself."

"And me. I am enchanted. Come dance with me." He held out his hand after offering an elegant bow.

Eugenia lifted her fan and bent to him in a confidential manner. He leaned with fascinated interest to hear her words.

"I am not well versed in dancing. I have just begun my lessons," she said with a conspiratorial whisper.

He was delighted, for he discerned no embarrassment at her confession. The ladies of his acquaintance would die a martyr's death before announcing such a failing.

"Then you have never danced with me. Come, I shall make you look as though you have been reared on a dance floor."

"You might regret it," she teased.

"Never! I have not been more entertained in months."

True to his boast, he led her flawlessly. His affinity to her translated into harmony, and they moved with matching grace. Eugenia was aware many eyes were on them, but he never let her falter.

"What is your name? I must know the name of the modest lady who dances like a princess," he said, taking her arm as they left the floor.

"I am Eugenia Winslow."

"Ah, the new Countess of Grahame. Now I understand his choice. I suspect the tittle-tattle I hear is quite incorrect. He is most fortunate, and, may I add, would be wise to not let you out of his sight. Come, I wish to present you to a friend."

She walked by his side as the guests opened a way for him in obvious deference, which she did not notice. Tittle-tattle? What was being said about her marriage? She wished she could ask. The frankness that had existed faded. She felt awkward again. She was about to ask him his name when they reached an admiring assembly clustered around the Prince of Wales.

"Your highness, allow me to present the most intriguing lady to grace London this Season," the gentleman said with a courtly bow. "The Countess of Grahame."

Eugenia presented the curtsy she had practiced under Blanche's eagle eye. "I am honored, your highness." She blushed.

"Ah, Grahame's bride. Welcome to our company. We are delighted to see Grahame has chosen so enchanting a lady. We are indebted to his valor. Where is he, by the way? I am vexed he has not called to receive my gratitude personally."

"Your highness, his wound is not completely healed. It is but eight months, and a ballroom is no place for him. He will be in London shortly, but not on a dance floor for some time yet." She did not know where the answer came from; it just popped out of her mouth. It was not far from the truth, but it was not the truth. She blushed at her pretext, but she could hardly say *Thomas preferred to be elsewhere.*

"But of course. Tell him he is commanded to present himself to me when he comes to London. I am eager to offer my gratitude for his bravery. England will prevail in our war with France with sons of his courage. Besides, as a military man myself, we will have much to speak about," he said with a flourish of his jeweled fingers. The prince fancied himself a military man, and there was none to refute his delusion, at least to his face.

He was magnificently dressed. Although portly, he carried a youthful expression on his face. His eyes were kind and his smile genuine. He was known for his affability, and Eugenia found herself at ease. "How do you find London?" the prince asked.

"Interesting, your highness, most interesting, an unending variety of sights and sounds. I must admit, however, a great part of my time has been spent in the shops. I hope to rectify that soon."

A trill of laughter ran through the guests standing with the prince.

"Spoken like a true member of the fair sex. We are pleased to have you among us. You and Thomas must dine with me at Carlton House when he arrives."

"We shall be honored, your Highness," she answered, and turned to move away, as she felt the conversation had come to an end.

"Your highness, excuse us. I am about to beseech this enchanting lady to grant me another dance. London will shine brighter this Season with so scintillating a star among us."

"How is it you always manage to find the most charming ladies with whom to dance? Your luck at cards should be as fortunate," the prince said, then laughed and the others, of course, joined him.

"I would agree, your highness. You must spend some time in conversation with the countess; no hand could compare."

The cluster of Court cronies who surrounded the prince joined in the laughter. Their eyes, however, reflected a new interest in Grahame's bride.

Eugenia took her place next to her partner on the dance floor just as the music began. She smiled at him when she began to follow with ease, knowing she did not look a novice.

"My lord, I think I may change my mind about merely seeking diversion. It is fun to dance when one can do so without stumbling. Thank you for introducing me to the joys of the ballroom," she said with a smile and a little curtsy at the end of the dance.

He placed her arm on his and said, "To whom do I return you?"

"Lord and Lady Sinclair, standing over there. But you must now tell me your name."

He walked with her across the room, then stopped and took her hand to his lips. "My dear enchanting child, you have just been brought into fashion by Beau Brummell."

She laughed. "Sir, I have enjoyed meeting you, whether I become fashionable or not. I shall smile each time I think about my first dance and the charming Beau Brummell."

He raised an eyebrow and joined her laughter. "I fear, I overrate my powers. I have no doubt; you would win the hearts of London on your own."

"I question that idea, but I do know it would not have been nearly as interesting. Why did you do it?"

"Why, my dear, I did it because it would make no difference to you whether or not I had. I knew you did not seek my company. It was I who sought yours. Tell Grahame, when he comes to London, I say he is the most fortunate of men." He kissed her hand again and left her in the company of her in-laws.

Brummell made his way back to the prince and his attending cronies. In his elegant hauteur he took no notice of the speculative glances. He took his place near the prince.

"She does not seem exceptional until you talk with her. Brummell, I do believe she owns the most spectacular eyes I have seen," Prinny said, looking in the direction of the new countess as she stood talking with Lord and Lady Sinclair.

"Would that fate had placed me in that snow-bank," Brummell said, taking an elegant pinch of snuff.

"Brummell, we do think you are smitten!"

"Only half in love, your highness, only half. I am a gambler, and believe in hedging all bets."

Prinny glanced up at his friend and sighed, for he of all people understood the pain of love. He again looked toward the countess and wondered what there was about her that could capture Beau.

Reading the prince's mind, Brummell added, "Can you imagine the joys of being married and never bored?"

The prince shuddered at the thought of his Caroline. "Do you think that is possible, Beau?"

"Only rarely. I think I have been fortunate enough to glimpse the possibility. Lady Luck has a wicked and capricious streak."

Twenty-one

Brummell paid a call on the Sinclairs and the Countess of Grahame the following morning. He handed his walking stick and hat to the waiting footman and was ushered into the drawing room, where Blanche and Eugenia were seated in anticipation of callers. He announced he had come to see if they had survived the rigors of the previous evening's ball.

Eugenia smiled as he bent over her hand. "My lord, you do not think we are so feeble as to let a little diversion tire us."

"Never, it is a lightly disguised excuse to see you again, and to invite Lord and Lady Sinclair and you to Vauxhall Gardens. That is, if you should enjoy the entertainments. I suggest the idea, for it is a remarkable place in which to view a myriad of people, actually of all walks of life."

"It does sound appealing. I think I should be right at home," Eugenia said with twinkle in her eye.

Brummell nodded. "Boswell can be quoted as saying 'Vauxhall Gardens is peculiarly adapted to the English nation; there is a mixture of curious show, gay exhibition, music, vocal and instrumental, not too refined for the general ear.' Knowing your interest in studying human nature, I suspect the sights might appeal to you." He chuckled at his quote, and those who knew the lofty Brummell would have been surprised to see him so pleased, for he was known for his cuts, not his humor.

He next bowed over Lady Sinclair's hand and asked if the evening suggested suited her plans. Blanche smiled and agreed it was a delightful idea. "Eugenia has not been to see Vauxhall, and I believe the first time is the most enchanting. Do you agree?"

"Then I am doubly fortunate. We will be joining a group of others, and if the weather holds, we shall enjoy a fine evening."

Brummell stayed no more than fifteen minutes and escaped when other callers arrived. Among those callers were Mrs. Rankin and her daughter, Lucy, who displayed an odious interest in the whereabouts of the earl. Blanche was relieved when the last visitor had gone.

Eugenia, for some strange reason, was merely amused by their inquiries. She was amazed at her detachment. Putting the idea away with the thought that she was now beginning to enjoy London and would not let pettiness spoil it, she looked forward to the evening.

It was dark when they entered the gardens. The broad avenue was planted with elm trees that branched over in a wide arch. Wooden arcades were covered with painted cloth and hung with colored lanterns that emitted a faint sweet smell.

They sauntered along the walk past the cascades of water to the center of the gardens, where the pavilion stood. This evening the orchestra pavilion was decorated with illuminations of the King of England and his Royal Crown. The lighting from the lanterns cast a glow so as to give the impression of rich enamel work. Music of a hundred musicians and singing voices came from the pavilion and could be heard throughout the gardens.

"It is like a fairyland! I never expected anything so lovely," Eugenia exclaimed.

"The night and the light is part of the illusion," Brummell added.

"I suspected as much, but the illusion is a wonderful sight."

A group of young dandies came strutting by, making catcalls after two young ladies hurrying away. They laughed and bounded through the sightseers with nary a thought to the jostling they incurred.

"You see, Countess, even here life intrudes on this illusion. Which reminds me to caution you: Never traverse one of the dark lanes. There are young blades about who think it great sport to prey on unsuspecting damsels."

Eugenia nodded, a little wide-eyed.

"Let us not dwell on the darker side of human nature," Brummell hastily added. "Come, we'll take our seats in the box and view the people as they promenade by."

After making introductions to the other members in the party, Brummell took his chair next to Eugenia. "You look very fetching this evening," he whispered. "I admire your style. You are wise to enhance your lovely eyes."

"Why, thank you. Coming from you, the compliment is high praise. I would only be redundant to say you are in prime fashion; nevertheless 'tis true."

He laughed. "You know perfectly well I make it my habit to be turned out to perfection. It has stood me in good stead for years."

"I understand you are generally considered formidable. I find you very comfortable," Eugenia said, and turned to watch the crowds pass by.

"That is the finest compliment I have ever received," he whispered.

"Really? Well, it's true."

Brummell sat back and a little frown crossed his brow. He quickly masked the expression. Grahame better get here soon, he thought.

The evening was a resounding success. Eugenia was delighted with every sight and sound. Brummell felt her enthusiasm and, for the first time in years, the excitement of the evening's entertainment.

The fireworks were spectacular. When any failed to reach high enough or went astray, squeals of delight or a call of "shocking" could be heard from the crowds. It was great fun.

The party left laughing and in high spirits. Eugenia had enjoyed the evening and hated to have it end.

"I shall remember this evening, forever. Thank you, Mr. Brummell."

"It was my pleasure. I will call again soon with another expedition, hopefully to entertain you."

"You are most kind. Thank you."

Eugenia bade him good night when they reached the Grahame town house. Lord and Lady Sinclair expressed their pleasure, and they all parted company with smiles.

* * *

Brummell continued to call at very discreet intervals. He always sought Eugenia out for at least one dance when they met at various parties. He arranged a few entertainments that included her. It was noted, he thought very highly of the lady, but he kept his distance enough to allow no improper speculations. He was very careful to keep their friendship so as not to bring unwelcome rumors. He did, however, let everyone know he thought her the belle of the Season.

He wanted to be the one to show her London and arranged to take her on a tour. First he took her to see St. Paul's. The day was cool and breezy when they set off. Brummell thought she looked very fetching in her sapphire pelisse and told her so.

"You are my friend; you need not cover me with drawing-room compliments."

"What if they are true?" he asked.

Brummell had spent his life complimenting or insulting to advance his reputation, and now when he was sincere he was accounted as making mere flattery. Well, he had earned that.

Eugenia was overwhelmed by the magnificent building. The view of the nave from the vestibule was breathtaking, and her steps slowed as they walked beneath the runs of arches toward the crossing. The dome over the crossing rose over the pilasters and windows with niches at intervals holding statues of the doctors of the church.

"They are the saints of the Western church, Saints Ambrose, Augustine, Jerome, and Gregory, and those of the Eastern church, Athanasius, Basil, Gregory of Nyssa, and Chrysostom. The fine mosaics in the spandrels depict the four evangelists, Mark, Matthew, Luke, and John."

"They are so beautiful!" she exclaimed, in awe of what man can accomplish.

Next he led the way up a magnificent spiral staircase to the Whispering Gallery. "The gallery derives its name from its excellent acoustics. A whisper at one side can be clearly heard at the opposite side one hundred feet away," Brummell explained.

"It is so beautiful, I cannot help the tears that threaten," Eugenia said.

"Come, let me show you the most sweeping view of London," he said, taking her arm and leading the way up a wooden ladder to a higher gallery. They could see London and the surrounding countryside for ten miles around.

"The houses and carriages look like toys. Oh, it is all beyond comprehension!"

The wind was cold, so they did not linger long. Next he took her to the Tower of London. He was a knowledgeable escort and regaled her with stories of every exhibit. She enjoyed every minute of the excursion and told him so.

"You are too kind. I merely wished you to see that London is not only a place to attend parties. It is full of history, and I would never tire of seeing the different sights. You could spend a lifetime, I think, and never fully comprehend it all."

"I have never enjoyed anything quite so much."

"Then it truly pleases me," he answered, and gave her hand a squeeze.

Invitations poured in, and Eugenia was besieged by young blades who wanted to count her among their dance partners. Blanche looked on with growing dismay.

Blanche could not decide if Eugenia was enjoying the attention, since she took it all without comment. Eugenia seemed to be marking time in a detached manner. Yet Blanche knew she took pleasure in some of the entertainments, and she knew she liked Brummell. Blanche found no fault there. Brummell usually included Lloyd and herself in their outings. She was troubled that Eugenia never mentioned Thomas, not once. That was it. It was as if Thomas did not exist.

Knowing she had best do something about this growing lack of interest, Blanche went to her secretary. Taking out pen and paper, she paused to think of just how to word her note in tones of cloaked urgency.

Thomas read Blanche's letter with alarm. He crumpled it in his fist and tossed it in the fireplace. Damn, he had meant only to give Eugenia time. Time to get accustomed to being a countess without his hovering over her. He had thought she could learn the ways of the ton, then meet him with the confidence so necessary to her. Her independence demanded no less.

He frowned. Damnation, if he wasn't wrong again! He should never let her out of his sight. She was young and maybe being the belle would turn her head. God knows, Brummell would turn any woman's head. He crossed the library and took the steps two at a time in his hurry to reach his bedchamber. He rang for Simmons, his valet.

"Pack my valise, I leave immediately for London."

* * *

The next evening Eugenia and Brummell were en route to the Sinclairs' town house after attending the opera and having a peek-in at the Duchess of Etherham's ball for her niece. They had attended the both events alone because Blanche had cried off, saying she was feeling unwell.

The streetlights flickered into the coach as it covered the distance. The rhythm of the horse's hooves clopping on the cobblestones was lulling. They sat in the comfortable silence of friends.

"I am going away for a few days, Eugenia. Do take care while I am gone," Brummell said, breaking the spell.

"Oh, I shall miss you."

"It is too much to hope you would, but people talk. It is time I absent myself from town for a few days."

"Talk? You are the paragon of virtue toward me. I thank you for making what would have been lonely days so enjoyable."

"Eugenia, I am half in love with you. I want no scandal to touch your name. Your marriage . . ."

"My lord, I never . . ."

"Exactly so. I have tried to protect you until that fool husband of yours arrives!"

"I am shocked."

"Nevertheless, it is so. My regard is too high, and I am afraid it shows."

"Oh, dear," she said, putting her fingers to her lips.

"Are you in love with Grahame?"

The question was like a slap. It made her focus on what she had tried to put out of her mind after the night Thomas made love to her. She realized just how abandoned she felt, and tears surfaced for herself and Beau.

"Yes, I am afraid I am."

"Afraid?"

"I do not think it is reciprocated."

"Then we both find ourselves in a pretty coil."

Silence fell between them, and they remained so until they reached the house.

They entered the hall, and Brummell took her hand in his. "Good-bye for a while. If ever you have need of me, I am at your service. You need only send for me." He kissed her hand and held it a moment, searching her eyes for what was not there.

"Good evening, Eugenia and Brummell, it is good to see you again." The low-timbred voice interrupted their exchange.

They started at the voice and turned to see Lord Grahame cross the foyer toward them. His icy gray eyes glittered no welcome.

"Thomas! When did you arrive?"

"A little while ago," he said, placing a peck of a kiss on her hair and reaching out to shake hands with Brummell.

Eugenia was furious. Livid! He had not let her know of his arrival. She would have gladly waited home for him. Well, there it was, plain as pudding. "I am tired, I shall bid my good night. Call on me when you return," she said sweetly to Brummell. She lifted her skirts and mounted the stair as regally as she could muster, never looking back.

Eugenia slammed the door to her bedroom and leaned against it. Her eyes were blazing. He treated her like an object to be noticed occasionally. Her breath came in gasps. She was the obligation she had never wanted to be. She had known this from the beginning, yet she just then saw what it really meant. Like a servant she was, to bide her time until she met his convenience. And then she was a disappointment to him.

"How can I spend the rest of my days like this?" she whispered to the empty room.

The two men watched Eugenia disappear at the top of the staircase. The hall was silent after the distant slam of a door. Brummell turned to take his leave.

"Come, come, have a brandy with me, Brummell. It has been ages since I last saw you." He placed a hand on Brummell's superbly tailored shoulder—few dared such an act—and guided him toward the library, where he had been having a nightcap and watching the fire. Actually, he had been waiting for Eugenia, but he would come to that later.

Exchanging pleasantries, the two men walked into the comfortable library. Thomas poured two brandies as Beau took a seat.

"Blanche tells me you have been very kind to my wife. I appreciate your interest."

"Like hell you do. Grahame, if a rooster doesn't have enough sense to watch his hen house, the fox will."

"You?"

"No such luck, old man. I merely watched out for her. She's an innocent in a world of knaves, myself included. Fate did not smile on me as she did on you. But, by God, I tell you, if Eugenia loved me, she would know she was loved in turn!" He put down his glass, rose, and moved to leave. He brooked no fools, least of all careless husbands.

"Know she was loved?"

"Close your mouth, Grahame, you look like the King's jester. Yes, she is in love with you, and for the life of me, I cannot figure it out." He opened the door and said, "No need to show me out, I know my way."

Thomas sat staring at the fire for a lost amount of time. Beau was right, he was a fool! She was everything he wanted, and he had dallied around for some stupid idea of gallantry. She had been on his mind the whole time he was alone at Windhaven. The nights had been pure hell. He longed to hold her again.

He remembered the fire in her eyes when he had greeted her. Anger showed some sort of attachment, and he was glad for it. Indifference would have killed him. She had a right to be angry with his leaving her, despite his intentions. Well, he thought, I shall rectify that.

Eugenia is about to be properly wooed! He did not know where to begin, but begin he would. Tomorrow he would win her love. He must! Life without her was dull and boring. He had missed her beyond measure. What a fool he had been. He should have realized his feelings sooner. He wanted to go to her now, but he had already gone that route. She deserved a proper courtship, and tomorrow he would begin.

Twenty-two

Eugenia entered their sitting room as passageway to her bedchamber. She had left the house early to avoid seeing Thomas and spent the day perusing lending libraries. She was busy untying her bonnet when she spied a leg hanging over the arm of the high wing chair that faced the fireplace. She stopped dead in her tracks.

"Is that you, my lord?" she asked, watching the leg disappear and the earl emerge. They stood looking at each other, each on the brink of speaking.

"It is, my dear." He offered a small bow and a hint of a smile.

She stood motionless, disarmed and annoyed, and the emotions marched across her face.

"What *marvelous* good fortune brings you to London?" she asked ever so "sweetly" when she, at last, found her voice and some semblance of thought.

"Sarcasm, Eugenia? Hardly a welcome for your husband."

She fidgeted with the ribbons of the bonnet, not knowing what else to say. He sailed in the previous evening with no forewarning or interest in seeing her. Shrugging, she moved toward her bedroom door. I shall say nothing, she thought, let him figure it out. Her feathers were mightily ruffled.

He moved like lightning and crossed the room quicker than she would have imagined he was capable. Placing his arm on her door, he stood towering over her while blocking her way.

She raised her eyes to him, and a moment of charged silence passed between them. She could not read his glittering eyes, but they made her uncomfortable. She moved to pass him, but he remained where he stood.

She raised her chin in defiance. "I am surprised to see you so soon. If I am surprised now, you can imagine my amazement last evening. Why are you here?"

"Why, to see my Jenny," he said, and a ghost of a smile crossed his lips. Hopefully, his bravado hid just how unsure he was.

"I am not your Jenny! I am not and never will be anyone's Jenny. She is a figment of a fertile adolescent mind. I admired her at the time only because she was pretty and smelled nice. I was neither. She represented stability and family, both sorely lacking in my life. If I could now be anyone in the world, it would not be a 'Jenny.' The spoiled darlings haven't a thought in their heads, and I would die of boredom trying to emulate such a creature."

"You are very pretty and you smell delightful, and I much prefer my Eugenia."

"Do you? Do you indeed? That is highly unlikely. I prefer your honesty to this false prattle. Now, let me pass!"

"Temper, temper. Aren't you going to kiss your husband, who has traveled all this way just to see your fair face, not to mention those flashing eyes?"

"I believe you gave me a passing kiss of greeting last evening, somewhere on my hair, I think."

"I am flattered you remembered, while Beau hovered at hand. Still, that was not the kiss I had in mind."

"Thomas, let me pass."

"Kiss me first. Consider it a toll fee."

"Thomas, I don't know you! Why are you behaving in this way?"

"Eugenia, you are exasperating me. Just kiss me hello. Is that too much to ask?"

She raised her face and puckered her lips. He reached over and pulled her to him. She felt his strong arms slide around her waist as he drew her tightly to him. Her breathing became uneven. She watched his face move closer and felt his mouth cover hers. She closed her eyes. The kiss sent a tremor through her body, and she leaned into him.

"Now, that is more like a dutiful wife," he said, drawing away. He opened her door and bowed with a flourish to indicate her passage.

She sailed by him with scarlet cheeks and a whirling mind. When she closed her bedroom door, she was positive she heard him chuckle. She clenched her fists. Damn the man!

While Eugenia was being helped into a reed of a gown in pale peach shot with silver thread, her mind traveled over the past few days. Thomas was totally vexing! She did not know what he thought. One minute he was loving, the next he takes off and leaves her to her own devices. Then he breezes in with no notice and expects *her* to welcome him as if any crumb of attention from him should be an utter delight. What else should she think? I ought to leave *him* to his own devices! She chuckled. Anything she would do was ineffectual; he would do as he pleased with or without her approval or presence.

She smoothed the gown and gazed at her reflection. Her eyes stared back in a wary manner. What was she expecting? A flutter stirred in her heart. She sent the unspoken thought away. She could play the same game as he.

Arranging the folds of her sleeves, she was satisfied with her appearance but shrugged at the thought, for it was not really important to her. And she was not going to pretend it was!

She glanced up in the mirror when the door to the sitting room opened and Thomas entered. He signaled her maid to leave. Maggie curtsied and scampered out.

Watching him cross the room in the reflection of the mirror, she turned to him when he reached her side. "I am ready to leave, my lord."

"I wish you would call me Thomas. I feel like a stranger when you say that. Or is it your wish to keep me at a distance?"

Her eyes narrowed and her fists tightened. She knew he was baiting her, and she struggled not to rise to the bait. "I cannot imagine what you are implying, Thomas."

"You can't, hmm. Well, here is a little gift that will be just the thing for that gown. You look ravishing, my dear." He removed a shimmering diamond necklace and draped it around her neck.

The cool metal and stones rested against her throat, and his warm fingers brushed her neck, sending a tingle down her spine. The diamonds sparkled on her bosom and seemed to call attention to the décolletage of her dress. She flushed. The neckline had not seemed so low before.

His hands tarried on her shoulders, then slid down her arms as he leaned over and placed a lingering kiss on her neck. "You look lovely, and the diamonds merely match your sparkle."

Eugenia moved away. "Is this some of your drawing-room manners? High-flying compliments?"

"Is that what you think?"

"I most certainly do! You abandon me in London and now act as though you are . . ."

"Are what, my dear?"

"Never mind. Let us leave. We do not want to be late for the ball."

His hand reached out and caught her arm. "Do you like the gift?"

"Oh, heavens, how ungrateful I must seem! Yes, it is gorgeous. Truly it is, thank you very much." She fingered the necklace and took one last look before moving to leave.

"No thank-you kiss?"

"Thank-you kiss? Thomas, you are acting very strange."

He reached over and drew her to him, just as he had the day before. His lips lingered with growing demand, and she tarried in his arms with an unbidden response.

The warmth spread through her body, and she realized once more she was at his slightest beckon. She placed her hands on his chest and pushed them apart, irate with her weakness to his kisses. What a traitor her emotions were. She was like some puppet while he pulled the strings.

Feeling the heat of her cheeks and trying to defuse the fiery moment, she tartly said, "That was more than the average thank-you kiss."

"You must admit, my dear, it is more than the average gift."

It was the Earl of Grahame's first appearance with his new wife, and many eyes turned with interest as they entered the lavish ballroom.

"We seem to be attracting more than a little interest," he whispered.

"They are simply amazed to see you at my side. I am sure the absence of Thomas Winslow has been under considerable speculation," she said caustically while displaying a smile.

He glanced sharply at her. So that *is* it, he thought. Despite her denials, she *does* resent my not staying and playing attendance on her in London. Now, that is a very good sign, he thought.

"Eugenia, why did not you tell me you desired me in London with you?"

"Desired you in London? What an odd notion," she quietly hissed just as Lord and Lady Russell approached them with greetings.

"Ah, Lord and Lady Russell. How nice to see you again," Eugenia gushed.

"Gratifying to see you are feeling better, Grahame. Time to enjoy London with your charming bride," Lord Russell said as he shook hands with Thomas. They stood, exchanging mere pleasantries, then passed on to greet others.

"So that is why you are acting so annoyed," he whispered as soon as he could.

"I am not acting annoyed. How would you like to go everywhere by yourself?"

"You had Blanche and Lloyd and the smitten Mr. Brummell."

"That's not what I mean!" She was about to elaborate when they were hailed by another couple eager to speak with Thomas.

"Admiral and Mrs. Dunning. How grand to see you," Eugenia said, and smiled to the couple bearing down on them.

"Grahame, old man. Good to see you. Met your charming wife already. We wondered where you had got yourself. It is grand to have you up and about again. Glad to see you set sail on the sea of matrimony with such fair weather."

"Eh, yes, Admiral. Fair weather indeed," Thomas replied, and turned to Eugenia. She tilted her head and smiled sweetly. She even batted her eyelashes.

"You minx, you told everyone I was ill?" he asked as soon as the admiral and his wife moved on to greet the others.

"What would you have me say? He does not enjoy being leg-shackled and departed back to Windhaven as soon as he could change horses?"

"That *is* why you are angry! I am flattered." He laughed at the idea.

"It is not amusing, my lord," she whispered.

"Well, at least I know why you have been acting the way you have."

"Acting? Now you tell me *I'm* acting. Sit down Eugenia, stand up Eugenia. . . . I do not *act.* I am not a puppet!" she snapped through her teeth, and began to fan her flushed cheeks.

Thomas was stunned by the passion of her anger. He had had no idea. Why had not she told him, or, more to the point, why had not he taken time to find out?

"Thomas! How grand to see you! You naughty boy. You didn't tell me you would be coming up to London so soon."

They both turned their attention to a fabulous beauty with an outstretched hand for Thomas to take in his. Thomas's eyes widened, and Eugenia's narrowed. She took in every detail of the elegant lady from head to foot in ten seconds flat.

"Eh, yes. Lady Linsey, may I present my wife."

"La, Thomas, how formal you are tonight." She tapped him on his arm with her fan in a mock chide. "So this is your bride. I am delighted to meet you." She glanced back to Thomas.

"Very charming and so young. You quite surprise me." She turned and rested her eyes on Eugenia. "You are most fortunate."

"How odd, that is exactly what Thomas is *always* saying," Eugenia answered with flashing eyes and a sweet, sweet smile.

"What does he always say?" Lady Linsey asked, not understanding Eugenia's meaning.

"How fortunate *he* is," Eugenia answered in wide-eyed innocence.

"Excuse us, please. There is someone I wish to present Eugenia to." He took his wife's arm and hustled her away as quickly as the crush of people would allow.

"That is very odd," Eugenia announced to his back as they squeezed single file through the throng, nodding to this person and that.

He turned. "What's odd?"

"That you didn't tell her *or* me you were coming up to London so soon."

"What in the hell does that mean?"

"Thomas, lower your voice! And it would suit my purposes if you would smile." She turned her back on him and greeted another acquaintance.

Where in the blue blazes did this termagant come

from? He was glad he had given her only a diamond necklace. Thank God, he hadn't chosen a matching bracelet or earrings! She'd have his head by now.

Just as Thomas was about to ring her neck, Eugenia was whisked away by some simpering gallant, and Grahame used the opportunity to escape to the card room. He hated cards. The admiral might wish fair weather, but it was rough seas tonight. He took up his hand. Damn, he'd never understand women.

Twenty-three

Eugenia scanned the crowded ballroom, and what had seemed so enchanting a few hours ago now appeared tawdry, garish, and artificial. While the glittering jewels, for the most part, were likely real, the laughter and bandied compliments were probably not. A jaded weariness swept over her.

Thomas was nowhere to be seen and she had not caught a glimpse of him in hours. Where had he gone? Not that she cared, she lied to herself. Putting her fan into motion, she sighed, for she was hot and tired, her feet ached, and her head throbbed. Some oaf jostled her, dripping punch down her dress. She needed fresh air or she would faint or die on the spot.

Where could Thomas be? she wondered, knowing she could hardly blame him for not playing attendance on her. What a wretch she had been. She had been rude and ugly to him, and her only justification was some vague thought that he was driving her to the boughs.

But she knew the reason she had reacted so fiercely. She was desperately in love with him. She finally admitted it to herself as she pushed her way through the crush. Who wouldn't be? She sighed in the pain and pleasure as love is wont to provide. If she just knew what to expect of him from one minute to the next, she could plan some strategy. He kept her off balance all the time.

She had remained passive waiting for whatever he would do next. She knew full well that was her inadequacy—until tonight. When she snapped back she had only reacted to him, never acting on her own thoughts.

She lacked the confidence to win Thomas, vacillating between emotions like a schoolgirl. Highly suspecting he was equally baffled by her actions, she smiled wickedly. She hoped he was as confused as she. A lowering thought came to mind, that he probably would not care.

Making her way through the press of people, her foot was again the object of an attack, and she was almost jolted off her feet. The heat grew more oppressive, and a feeling of vertigo assailed her. What I would give to be at Windhaven now! Away from all this! She headed toward the doors that led to the terrace and the heavenly promise of fresh air with a newly planted seed of an idea in her mind.

"I'm out, gentlemen," Thomas said, tossing down his hand and rising from the card table. A pain shot through his leg, and it felt stiff from sitting so long. To add to his discomfort, it was hotter than hell. Leaving the game room, he scanned the throng for Eugenia, but she was nowhere to be seen. He headed toward the french doors leading to the terrace and some cool air.

"Thomas, escort me out for some fresh air. I am about to faint from this heat."

An icy flicker crossed his eyes as he turned and

saw Lady Linsey grinning up at him like a cat looking into a fishbowl. His skin crawled.

"How unkind of you to frown so. I only seek some fresh air, and it would be delightful to speak of old times," she said with what she was sure was an enchanting smile.

It would be rude to decline, so he reluctantly took her arm and they crossed to the balustrade at the edge of the terrace. The cool air was wonderfully refreshing.

"I was delighted to run into you last week," Lady Linsey said with a delicate flutter of her lashes more suited to the ingenue. "I had meant to call upon you to see how you were mending, when I heard of your marriage," she said with a small sigh that indicated regret.

"I have been home from the Peninsula for months."

"Well, yes, but I had hoped to see you again. Since Edward's death . . . it's been so lonely. . . ." She allowed her words to trail away in "unspoken sorrow" as she gazed up at him with an open invitation in her eyes.

"Highly unlikely," he replied tersely.

"You've never thought of me?"

"My God, it has been years! Frankly, no. When you married Edward, I figured you had made your choice. Besides, I was in my salad days."

"Thomas, I never forgot you." She placed her arm on his and stepped closer. He pushed up against the balustrade and could not step back.

"That is your problem. You made your choice," he said, contemplating how he could peel her off his arm.

"It was my family, Thomas. They insisted."

"It was Edward's money and title. My title lay years in the future."

"You did care!"

"Only a little, for even less time." He gently moved her aside and started to pull away.

"But you never married. I always thought it was because of me."

"You were wrong, and I have now," he said, his voice carrying a warning.

"But is it your choice? I quite understand that you were doing the honorable," she insisted as only one can who sees nothing beyond her own interest.

Thomas's eyes narrowed. "Yes, by God. She is my choice . . . from the first day I saw her. . . ." His voice faded, and a wretched expression crossed his face. "If you will excuse me, I must go find my wife."

Unfortunately, Eugenia stood watching the intimately whispered conversation between Thomas and that lady. Seething, she slipped back into the ballroom, where Thomas found her some moments later.

"So, I finally locate you. I've come to take you to supper, unless, of course, some swooning gallant has claimed the honor," Thomas said, raising his arm for her to take.

"Thomas, take me home. I have a headache."

The carriage ride home was as ominous as a smoldering powder keg. He noted her occasional searing glance and the defiant lift of her chin. What a prickly pear she was. He hid his amusement and sat in silence.

When they entered their apartments, Eugenia

moved quickly toward her door. He reached out and caught her arm.

"You have been angry with me all evening. Tell me why."

She shook off his arm. "Why? Why? You tell me why! You answer that."

"Eugenia, I gave you the necklace to show you—"

"Take it back and give it to your friend with the bounteous . . . eh . . . bosom!"

"Bosom?"

"Yes, the one draped over you on the terrace." Eugenia put her hands on her hips and tapped her foot.

"Oh, that one," he said, and smiled. "You are jealous! At last I get somewhere; that is a good sign."

"I most certainly am not. Good night."

He reached for her again. "Come kiss me."

She stopped and stared at him. "I am not your sweetheart; I am the obligatory wife, remember."

"Eugenia! There is nothing between Lady Linsey and me. And what of Brummell at your beck and call these past weeks?"

"Brummell? He is a friend. Belive me, I could use one. Besides, he likes me the way I am!" she said, her voice rising. She knew her stylish gown and acquired graces had first attracted Beau, but she wasn't going to admit that.

"Not as much as I do," he said quietly, and crossed his arms as he leaned against her door frame.

"Really? Well, it gratifies me to know I turned out to your liking. I have been bidden into a mold. Learn to dance. Learn to walk. Cut your hair. Wear this, say that. Well, this is the result. I hope you are happy!"

"Only if you are."

"Well, I'm not!" Tears filled her eyes.

He reached out, drew her to him, and leaned his head toward her.

"Don't patronize me, Thomas. We made a bargain. I'll try to keep it. Good night." She shoved out of his embrace. He let his arms drop. He stood back and gave her passage.

"Good night," he said quietly to the slamming door.

Fighting back tears, Eugenia allowed Maggie to help her out of the ball gown, then quickly dismissed her. As soon as she was alone the tears trickled down her cheeks. She fingered the lovely necklace and knew she had been ungrateful and unkind. She had been driven by her anger. It had gotten ahead of her, and she had vented all her pent-up indignation on her reluctant husband.

Why such anger? she wondered. But she knew the answer. She was a pawn in a world she little understood. She was in love with her husband, while he had been coerced to marry her. He had tried to show kindness, and she had lashed out. Why? She did not want kindness, which she suspected was prompted by pity, because she could not face loving and not being loved in return. A bed partner did not mean love. She wept. Her brave words that she would keep her bargain rang in her ears, for she knew now she would never be able to do so. Her overwhelming love would lead to heartbreak. Better to put him off now than suffer greater hurt later.

She had always been at the command of some

man's decision. Most women were. How did they abide it? She could not compromise, and she would lose the man she loved because of it. Tomorrow I will go to Windhaven, she vowed. London society was not to her liking; she would pretend no longer. Thomas would be glad to see her go after her outrageous behavior tonight.

Thomas won't stay in London; he will go to Windhaven, she realized. Then she would go and live at the hunting box. She might be lonely, but less so than here in London or being with him at Windhaven. She cried herself to sleep.

"Damn, damn, damn," he muttered aloud, and kicked a chair over in childish, frustrated anger. It knocked against the table, sending an exquisite Sevres vase crashing to the floor.

What a wicked temper Eugenia had! From out of the blue it had come. No warning and certainly no provocation. He had shown her nothing but kindness. He had been trying to woo her slowly, not rushing his traces, but he was failing miserably. He ought to go and declare his feelings, and demand his marital rights.

Most husbands, he decided, would not make such a fuss. They would simply demand their rights and consider the deed done to their satisfaction. His heart constricted. He wanted more from Eugenia, much more.

He had lived in a household where his parents did not love each other. His father had never been home and his mother was usually in London enjoying the pursuits of society. He had not rushed to marry because he wanted to find someone who valued family life as much as he did. Eugenia, who had spent many years alone in an orphanage, would surely do so. He knew they would get on perfectly if he could just figure out what to do. What if he came out with it and said I love you? Under the circumstances of their marriage, he was afraid to risk that. If he could just win her by wooing her, but he had not scored well on his efforts so far.

If he were in the army still, he could order her to love him. He stopped in his tracks. This last thought proved beyond a doubt that he was not only going around the bend, he already had. Eugenia had a way of doing that to him. She was driving him to distraction. If he could get her in bed again . . . but he did not want to demand his rights, he wanted her to come willingly. The chances of that were growing slimmer by the day. His "deft" handling of the situation was proving to have the touch of an oaf.

Thomas was beside himself. He paced up and down the room, frowning, mumbling to himself and now and again shaking his head. He was making a cake of himself. He was not the romantic-lover type. He could not continue chasing her around, begging her for kisses. When he tried to act the lover he merely managed the fool.

Why in hell is it harder to woo one's wife than it is a stranger? That was the devilish part! He had never had any problem getting a lady into his arms and now he was helpless. He ought to wring her neck. He had done everything humanly possible to please her, and now she is fit to be tied. Women were totally impossible, and she was the queen of them all!

She had given him no encouragement. Yet, it was true, she melted in his arms. He knew perfectly well she liked his kisses, but sexual attraction did not mean she loved him. Was he a fool or just a coward? Both, his mind seemed to whisper.

The diamond necklace had been a failure. He should have known she would not go into raptures over it. Actually, that was one of the very reasons he loved her, so why had he thought to woo her with jewels? What could he give her to let her know what he was trying to get the courage to say?

"The one thing she would want! I have it!" he said with triumph. A broad smile appeared. All was fair in love and war, and he would win this one yet.

Late in the night Eugenia awoke. She wanted to go to Thomas. She needed him, his comfort, and his strength. She started to move. She paused, only a hussy would go so boldly to a man's bed, or so she had been told.

Quietly, she stared into the dark room. She would go anyway and tell him how she felt. This time she moved the covers off and began to leave the bed. No, she couldn't do it! Quickly and embarrassed, she snuggled back under the covers.

She remained huddled for a few moments. No, she would go! This time she got as far as putting her feet on the floor. What if he was shocked? Refused her? Maybe he did not want her in his bed. He had not made an effort to seek her since . . . She quick hopped back in bed. She could not do it! She could not risk rejection.

"Tomorrow I will leave. That is the only answer. Leave or go round the bend," she said to the silent room.

Twenty-four

With constant admonitions for silence from Eugenia, Maggie managed to secure a trunk from storage at this ungodly hour. Dawn had only begun to creep across the sky with the palest of gray light from the eastern horizon. The two women dragged the trunk across the carpet and into Eugenia's room. They set about packing for Eugenia's journey.

Until the moment her ladyship had roused her from sleep, Maggie had not even heard of a journey. The surreptitious way in which they carried the trunk and hat boxes to the room gave Maggie an uneasy feeling. She prayed his lordship would not have her sacked for aiding and abetting what obviously was being done secretly.

"Take only what I need for the country. No fancy ball gowns. Pack only what is necessary and only enough to fill this one trunk," Eugenia commanded.

Maggie nodded, but her heart stayed in her throat.

With the utmost care Eugenia dressed for breakfast in a dimity morning dress while she had Maggie lay out her smart green traveling attire with the black braid and frogs.

"But how, my lady?" Maggie whined with fear.

"Tell them I'm not well and want to rest!"

"While you've gone to breakfast?"

"Yes. Tell them I want to rest after breakfast and do not want my room disturbed."

"Yes, my lady," Maggie said with a curtsy and a perplexing expression.

"Above all else, do not tell anyone what we have been doing!"

Maggie nodded, her heart dropping. She just hoped she would not be blamed for assisting her mistress. Wringing her hands, she recognized a no-good-will-come-of-it situation when she saw it. She sighed. Her duty was to her mistress and she would keep anyone from entering the room.

When Eugenia entered the breakfast room, everyone was seated and happily chatting.

"Good morning, Eugenia," Blanche said.

"Good morning, my dear. I trust you slept well?" Thomas asked, rising and helping her into the chair on his right.

"Yes, my lord. Like a lamb," Eugenia lied.

"Then you fared far better than I," Thomas said.

Eugenia met his eyes and her heart skipped, for he looked tired and worried. Oh, dear. It is best I get away. I am bringing him nothing but misery. She stared at her plate. How did she answer his remark? It was best to let it go by.

"We were just discussing our departure tomorrow," Blanche said.

Eugenia looked up in surprise. "So soon?"

"Eugenia, I have allowed Blanche to be away too long. I miss her when she's not at Tower House. London is lovely for a while, but it is time for us to return," Lloyd said, sending an intimate glance to his wife.

"Oh, yes, of course. You all have been so kind to see me along my way in the intricacies of the ton. I shall miss you, of course." Eugenia's words seemed to fall out in a mumble.

The conversation concerned the Sinclairs' departure, and Eugenia listened with a pasted smile on her lips, hoping none would notice her nervousness. Other than that, she kept her eyes on her plate and toyed with her food. She was afraid to look at Thomas, lest he read her intentions in her eyes.

"Eugenia, I must leave for a day but I shall return on the morrow. There is a matter of utmost importance that I must attend. I will return before nightfall tomorrow," Lord Grahame said while watching her reaction. He frowned—she seemed relieved!

"That is agreeable, my lord," she said with too much enthusiasm. "I shall like a quiet day and evening. I am exhausted from all our recent activities. A good night's sleep is exactly what I need," she said, and turned an innocent smile on him.

"I thought you just had one."

"Oh, exactly so. I need another," she hastily added.

Thomas looked at her with piqued interest, for he felt an underlying warning and wondered at her manner. He shrugged. He doubted he would ever understand her.

With incredible luck the stage was set exactly to Eugenia's liking. It could not have worked out better. She saw Thomas off at the front door, then swiftly called the butler. "Have the traveling coach brought around in an hour."

"Madam?"

"You heard me. Have the traveling coach brought around in an hour. I also require a basket of food for a luncheon in the coach, if necessary."

"As you wish, my lady."

It was only a short time later that Eugenia, dressed in her traveling gown, sought out Blanche.

"Eugenia! Where are you going?"

"Blanche, may I speak with you privately?"

"But of course, dear. Come, we'll find privacy in the library."

After seating themselves, Blanche waited for Eugenia to broach whatever topic she had in mind and feared for the worse.

"Blanche, I am going to Windhaven today. I must get away from London."

"Does Thomas know of your intentions?"

"No."

"I see. He will find out in time. What do you hope to gain by this, and why are you doing it? Has he been unkind to you?"

"No, he has been most kind. I just could not bring myself to tell him to his face. I am a coward. Oh, Blanche, it is such a mess and a terrible mistake."

"What is?"

"I should never have married him. I knew better, but you see . . . I really . . ."

"Love him?"

"Blanche, does it show?"

"To some, but I doubt Thomas has seen it. If you love him, why would you run away?"

"I am not running away. I am going to Windhaven to think."

"About what?"

"Oh, Blanche, you just don't understand."

"I understand far more than you do. I will tell you this. I have never seen two such stupid and stubborn people in the world as you and Thomas. Believe me, you deserve each other."

"Stupid and stubborn?" Eugenia asked, a little more than aghast.

"And cowardly!"

"Blanche! I was foisted on him. He does not love me. Oh, he has tried to make a go of it, but I know he feels trapped."

"You do? Your perception is sorely lacking. Do you think for one minute that Thomas would wed where he did not want?"

"For honor?"

"He could have found you a husband if he had wanted out. There would have been no scandal if you had been quietly married off to a country squire."

"You think he married me because he wanted to?"

"I don't think he had come quite that far. I know he did not want you married to someone else. He came back from the journey enamored with you. He was intrigued. He is as stubborn as you, and it took him a while to see it. He's been in love with you since he brought you home."

"If that is so, why didn't he tell me?"

"Do you love him? Have you told him?"

"Yes, no."

"Why not?"

Eugenia sat, incredulous. Her mind whirled. She did not believe it and yet there was a wee voice that said it might be so.

"Eugenia, Thomas has made his life until now in the army. He is not versed on the ways of female society, for I truly believe he was more interested in his career. He needs encouragement. I believe he is equally afraid of declaring his love as you are. In some ways, your lives have much in parallel."

"Blanche, I have to go. I will think over what you have said. But I must go."

"Why?"

"I am afraid my love is greater, and I shall be hurt with his rebuff."

"What rebuff? Has he done so?"

Eugenia began to cry. "Blanche, it is all just too scary. I must go to Windhaven."

"He will follow."

"Then perhaps I will risk telling him how I feel."

"By the Great Eternal, let us hope so. The melodrama is a bit much."

Eugenia had the grace to laugh.

It was past midnight when Eugenia and Maggie arrived at Windhaven. The servants, who had been awakened to help their new mistress, were taken by surprise. No one had told them to expect the countess, and they bustled about to accommodate her. It was most unusual that a servant had not been sent on ahead to warn of an impending arrival.

A warming pan was placed in her bed and a fire hastily lit in the hearth to ward off the chill of the closed bedchamber. Hot tea and a light repast were placed in her room. With warnings not to disturb the countess come morning, they retired, shaking their heads at the whims of their new mistress.

Eugenia, exhausted by her journey and her emotions, slept until noon. She spent the afternoon reading and went to bed early. Thomas was never far from her thoughts even when she vowed to put him from her mind.

The rest was doing her good. She took long walks in the garden and even ventured to the stables for a peek at the horses.

Still, her mind would insist on thinking of Thomas. She missed him. She simply did not know what he felt toward her. She even dared to hope Blanche was correct.

Retiring early again, she drifted into a deep sleep until she heard sounds in the hall. Her eyes fluttered open and she lay listening. It seemed the servants were again roused from their sleep. She sat up. Thomas had arrived, she was sure. She waited, wondering if he would come to her room, but he did not.

Her reprieve was over. She would have to face him tomorrow. Snuggling back into her pillow and covers, she wondered what she should do. She knew she would again play the coward and wait to see what he did or said. She simply could not blurt out her love for him.

Sleep did not return, and she spent the rest of the night imagining various scenes between them on the morrow. She tried to end them happily, but her mind refused to do so. Tomorrow would dictate its own events, and nothing she could do would change that. Unless, of course, she were willing to take the risk and declare herself.

Twenty-five

Lord Grahame rode out early in very high spirits. One could see the gleam in his eye, the smile on his lips, and the jaunty set of his shoulders. Sure the glorious day was an omen to his plans, he galloped with gleeful abandon across the fields. He was carefully setting the plans for his final assault in the wooing and winning of his wife. He was confident the day would be his.

First, he had been angry when he had returned to London to find Eugenia had gone to Windhaven, but now that fit very nicely into his plans—very nicely, indeed.

He chuckled quietly to himself. Let her have her flight; it was only a matter of hours now. He would take the offensive, and the field would be his. He was sure of it. A woman who was indifferent would not run from her husband. A woman who hated her husband might, but Eugenia did not hate him. Her kisses told him that. He had dilly-dallied too long in some misguided sense of chivalry.

He headed his horse toward the hunting box, having left his instructions with his valet to administer.

* * *

Eugenia was quite surprised not to find Thomas about. She had dressed with enormous care for their encounter. "His lordship has gone out. He has instructed me to tell you he will see you for dinner," the butler informed her with more than casual interest when she descended the steps and headed for the dining room. She blushed and hated herself for it.

The day dragged on endlessly. She tried to read, only to find herself staring at the page. She walked in the garden and that soon paled, because she kept glancing around in anticipation of Thomas's arrival. She jumped at every sound, expecting Thomas to appear. And when he did not, her heart plunged in disappointment. It was most unnerving, and she became annoyed with herself. She was playing right into his hands, waiting around like a ninny. Still, she waited.

While the sun cast low rays across the land, Eugenia went to her room to prepare for dinner. It was apparent she was not going to see Thomas before the meal. She would settle once and for all with him just what their life together would be. She was not going to spend her life on tenterhooks, waiting for him to make up his mind.

She chose a peach silk gown of the simplest design. It was an elegant cut and enhanced her hair and eyes. She fastened the diamond necklace around her neck and studied her reflection. The diamonds were a bit much, but she hoped Thomas would take it as a tribute to him.

She looked at her reflection. A lady of fashion had replaced the waif. She had gained weight, which had softened her gaunt look with feminine curves. All in all she was very pleased. She needed to make no excuses for some perceived lack. She would do, and do very well. This translated into a confidence of carriage that was extremely attractive.

Maggie answered the soft knock at the door. "Tell your mistress the carriage is ready," a footman said.

Eugenia glanced toward Maggie, who nodded. "His lordship has asked that you dine with him at the hunting box."

"I am the last to know?" Eugenia said, then bit her tongue. It was best to say as little as possible to the servants, even one's maid.

Maggie placed Eugenia's cape about her shoulders and wished her a happy evening.

"Shall I wait up, madam?"

Eugenia paused. "No, Maggie. I shall not need you tonight." Her heart gave a flutter, and she smiled to herself. Perhaps tonight she would initiate events rather than wait for Thomas to set their direction.

Eugenia entered the parlor of the charming hunting box, and memories of her earlier visit flashed across her mind. The same girl did not cross the threshold, and she was ever grateful of that fact.

A fire danced merrily in the hearth to stave off the cool night air, and it cast a warm glow on Thomas's face.

"Come, have a bit of sherry," he said, pouring some into the fragile glass.

Slipping off her cape, she moved slowly across the room while studying every detail. The table set for two by the fire and decorated with spring flowers and flickering candles recalled her wedding day. "How very charming. Your idea?"

He chuckled, remembering the same remark he had given her. "Yes, and since it is such a good one, I could not resist."

"Hmm," she murmured as she took the proffered glass.

"You look lovely, Eugenia."

She raised an eyebrow, but she realized he meant what he said. "You look equally grand, my lord."

"Why did you go off without telling me where you were going?" he asked.

"I merely emulated you, my lord," she replied very sweetly.

"I told you I was going for a short time."

"But not where, my lord. And besides, you were not there to tell."

Things were not going well. He absently felt the folded paper in his breast pocket. He smiled when he knew, for the hundredth time, it was safely tucked away.

"I am glad you are here, Eugenia. I find myself . . ."

Servants arrived to place the dinner on the table to be used as a sideboard. Rich aromas sent a pang of hunger to Eugenia, and she watched as they spooned out the rich oyster stew.

"Thomas, it is the very same dinner as—"

"I thought it might please you."

"It surprises me . . . that . . . you remembered."

"Believe me, I quite surprise myself," he said, and chuckled with the surprise he carried in his breast pocket.

While the meal was delicious, the conversation was commonplace. Weather was thoroughly exhausted, and long periods of silence spelled the vapid remarks.

Lord Grahame watched the servants finish clearing away the dinner and quietly close the door. He turned to Eugenia and smiled, feeling a little nervous about presenting his latest effort at wooing his wife. His hand touched his coat, and he moved to take a chair next to Eugenia.

Eugenia started to rise. "The dinner was delicious. I am tired, so I think I'll retire."

"Stay, Eugenia." He took a folded document from his inside breast pocket. He fingered it and seemed to hesitate. "I have a gift for you. I hope you will like it, since it could be considered bizarre, although that is not my intention." He hoped she would understand his intention as he handed the official-looking document to her and sat back, waiting and watching. He was not surprised at his apprehension. He wanted her to know what he had not yet said. He needed some indication from her, and he held his breath.

Eugenia looked puzzled as she opened the folded parchment. Her eyes scanned the written words, and her expression began to change from puzzlement to recognition. She gasped, then looked up at her husband.

"You did this for me?"

"Does it please you? That is my ambition."

She burst into tears.

Thomas was aghast! "Good Lord, I've failed again," he said, moving to her.

"Oh, no, Thomas. I cannot believe it! It is too wonderful!"

"Then why are you crying?" he said, lifting her

to her feet while she shed her tears in loud choking sobs.

"These are happy tears," she said, and cried even harder on his exquisite coat.

Would he ever understand women? he wondered.

"That was my purpose, to make you happy, but don't cry."

"I know, I know, but I am so happy." She struggled to stay her sobs.

He kept his arms around her and murmured soft words she did not understand. She laid her head against his chest, and he stroked her hair. They remained so until she brought her tears under control.

"What shall I do with it?"

"Why, whatever you wish. First dismiss the Smythe woman, then staff it with competent people. See that it is properly run, and the children have all they need in the way of attention and love."

Her tears began again. "I could do that! I could make all the children's lives so much better. Oh, Thomas, you are wonderful. Thank you so much!"

A flood of relief swept through his being as he pulled her close.

She looked up at him and asked, "But why?"

"Don't you know?"

"I do not know. I never know what to expect from you. One minute you make love to me and the next you abandon me."

She looked into his eyes and saw a tenderness that brought a flood of emotion that again threatened to emerge in tears. She rested her head again against his chest.

"How shall I be worthy?"

"What do you mean?"
"How can I deserve such kindness?"
He put his hands on her shoulders and pulled away slightly. He gently stroked her cheek.
"Eugenia, I love you. I have loved you since the beginning." He bent down and kissed her wet cheek and then moved to her full, inviting mouth.
"Oh, Thomas, do you?"
"I told you so. Did I stay away too long?"
"I am afraid so. . . ."
"I wanted you to find your way. You are capable of so much. I did not want you to be a shadow beside me."
"What a silly reason to leave me alone."
"I love you, adore you! Eugenia, do not keep me in trepidation. Can you, do you, reciprocate my feeling, even just a little?"
"Oh, Thomas, it is too much. I have loved you since the crofter's cottage." She raised her face again and enthusiastically returned his kisses.
After a few moments spent in exchanged kisses, Eugenia suddenly pulled away. "Are we complicating a perfectly good marriage with love?"
"But of course. Love makes us all vulnerable. It has made me a virtual oaf in trying to convey my feelings."
"Thomas, how is it me? You could have the choice of all the beautiful rich ladies of the ton? I know you were coerced into marrying me, but how can it be you could love me with so many from which you could choose?"
"You overrate my charm, my dear. But then, love is blind. There is none to match you. From the moment you raised those glorious eyes to me, I was lost. As far as being forced to marry you, do you

seriously believe I would have married you had I not wanted to? I will admit, I fought it for some time but then, that is not unusual for perennial bachelors."

"Thomas, I still think I am dreaming. Kiss me again so I know I'm not."

He obliged his wife.

"Are you sure this is not all because I bought a school for you?" he teased while trailing his kisses to her neck.

"My lord, you know better than that!"

"Do I? Then prove it to me."

"Yes, my love, I intend to, and I intend to continue being outrageous where you are concerned."

He swept her up into his arms. He had won. The victorious warrior carried her to his bed with joyful strides. He gently and tenderly laid her on his bed while continuing to kiss her. Her arms slid around his neck, and she drew him to her. She was so soft and warm, snuggled in his arms. His heart nearly burst with happiness. His hand slid to the tiny buttons on the back of her silky gown.

"Wait. Stop, Thomas, I have to get something."

It was like a slap as he came to understand what she was saying. "Stop? Are you mad?"

"No. Just a moment," she said, slipping from his embrace and off the bed. Her hair and gown looked enchanting in disarray. "I shall be right back. Wait for me."

Wait for her! "Eugenia, where in hell are you going?"

She leaned over him and kissed him. "Thomas, just a moment. I shall return. Blanche gave me a beautiful nightdress for our first night together. I was too shy to wear it. Since this is our real beginning, I intend on coming to you looking like the bride you deserve."

"Eugenia, I intend to remove it as soon as I can."

"That, my lord, is your privilege—and my pleasure," she said provocatively, then disappeared through the door.

He rolled on his back. Life with her will never be dull. The future looked more promising than he had dared to dream. He had hoped for the day when she would come to him willingly. He could hardly believe his good fortune.

Imagine how close he came to never knowing her! Fate had decreed their meeting, for it would never have been so but for the fact of a guardianship and a snowstorm.

His musings ceased when Eugenia came back into his room and softly closed the door. Wearing a cloud of white silk and lace, she came to stand next to the bed and smiled as sweetly as an angel.

He caught his breath. "My love, you take my breath away." He held out his arms.

Joyfully, she climbed in bed and bounced into his waiting arms. "What a lovely way to begin our marriage," she said, and waited to receive his lusty kiss.

"Far be from me to correct you, my dear, but it began when you crossed that cold priory hall and raised your captivating eyes to me."

"I thought you did not like me. You had such a frown!"

"I was hearing the death knell of my single state."

"Whatever you say, my lord."

"Kiss me."

She obeyed.